# HORSEMEN OF THE APOCALYPSE

## A Comedy for the End times

### First Edition

# NITKA MARGA

Illustration on the cover designed by SoulBound Books using Canva. For permissions inquiries, please contact: SoulBound Books LLC
Printed by Amazon KDP

**ISBN: 979-8-9891265-0-7**

First Edition
2023

**www.soulboundbooksinfo.com**

SoulBound
BOOKS

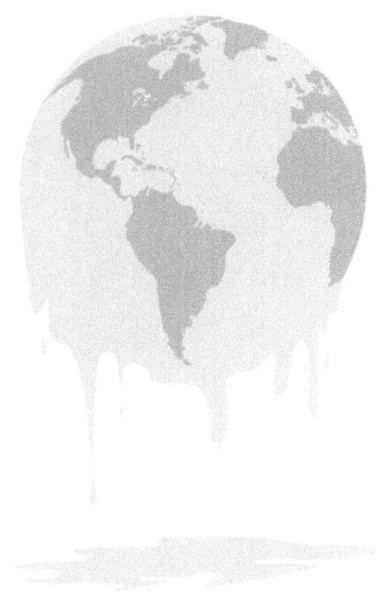

NITKA MARGA

# Dedication

To the Unsung Hero of the Apocalypse,

In the intricate tale of the end times, there exists a figure whose contribution often goes unnoticed, yet its significance remains irreplaceable. This book is dedicated to the one who, with unyielding commitment, undertakes a task both unglamorous and essential—the devoted soul responsible for maintaining cleanliness of the horsemen's horses while they wait to usher in the apocalypse.

Let us indulge in the hypothetical scenario that the four heralds of chaos indeed exist and have been patiently waiting for their moment to reign for the past two millennia. As we contemplate this, consider the daily excretion habits of horses, known for their undeniable regularity. Multiply the average daily excretions of a horse by four—the number of horsemen—and the staggering quantity of waste that this uncelebrated hero has managed becomes apparent.

Yes, it's a somewhat crude contemplation, yet it serves as a tribute to the dedication of someone who has valiantly shouldered the less glamorous responsibilities of the impending doom. While the world trembles at the thought of apocalyptic circumstances, this steadfast individual deals with it as part of their routine. Each shovelful and every wheelbarrow they've wielded embodies both gritty determination and a unique form of heroism.

Here's to the one who embraces the less poetic, more pragmatic aspects of the impending cataclysm—a guardian who remains vigilant as the world casts its gaze on grander narratives. Your diligence may be concealed behind the scenes, but it hasn't gone unnoticed. While we hypothesis about the potential arrival of the apocalypse, it's with your well-being in mind that we might even wish for its hastened conclusion.

**For the Being Who Has Been Shoveling Horse Shit for Two Millenia. We Applaud You.**

"Life is a comedy for those who think and a tragedy for those who feel."
- Horace Walpole

# List of Characters

**Ezriel:** The supernatural mentor responsible for initiating the apocalypse.

**Elara:** The agent of famine among the Four Horsemen of the Apocalypse.

**Morten:** Embodies death and is one of the Four Horsemen.

**Seraphel:** Master of conquest and a member of the Four Horsemen.

**Cassain:** The harbinger of war, also among the Four Horsemen.

**Liora:** Ezriel's assistant.

**Larry:** The apocalyptic street preacher.

**Ben:** Some guy from New England

# CHAPTER 1

# THE APOCALYPTIC
# STREET PREACHER

The heart of the city was its bustling streets, where pedestrians of all kinds traversed, and today, they were treated to an unusual spectacle. Larry, the Apocalyptic Street Preacher, stood atop a soapbox, waving a well-worn Bible and warning all who would listen about the imminent arrival of the Four Horsemen.

"The end is nigh! Carpe Diem! The Four Horsemen are coming!" Larry's voice cut through the urban landscape.

From among the growing crowd, a child, face etched in genuine curiosity, raised a question. "So, are the horses like... horse-sized? Or bigger? Because if they're horse-sized, I don't see how that's very apocalyptic."

Larry, momentarily taken aback, responded, "They are horse-sized. But they fly, which makes them very apocalyptic."

A passerby yelled from the window of their car, "Good luck finding parking for these flying horses!"

Ignoring him, Larry soon found himself confronted by a teenager, engrossed in her smartphone. "Do the Horsemen have social media? I'd love to follow them for some end-of-the-world content."

The child returned, this time with a curious thought, "How do they fly?.. Do they have rocket boosters? Like in my video games?"

"No! They don't have rocket boosters! Maybe they have wings, alright?" Larry responded, flustered.

"But if they have wings, then they are like Pegasus, right?" the child pointed out, looking smug.

"No they're not Pegasus! They're horses!" Larry's patience was visibly fraying.

An elderly lady, with a nostalgic look, reminisced, "Back in my day, horsemen rode real horses. No flying nonsense!"

A couple, holding recyclable coffee cups, questioned, "Are the horses sustainably fed? I mean, with all this end-of-the-world stuff, we still need to think of the planet."

Another young man in the crowd raised his hand. "Do they do, like, a show? Can I get tickets?"

Growing increasingly frazzled, Larry attempted to steer the conversation. "No! They don't perform a show, and they're not Pegasus. They are flying horses, and they're going to destroy us all!"

Three hipsters nearby began to chat among themselves. "I knew about the Four Horsemen before they went mainstream," one of them bragged.

"Oh yeah, their stuff is dope," replied another.

Larry interjected, "What?! No! They're not a band; they're going to destroy us all!"

The third hipster added, "Let them destroy this beat," and played some music from his vintage boombox. The trio began to dance, drawing laughter from the crowd.

A jogger, pausing to catch his breath, interjected, "When is this going to happen?"

Larry replied, "Soon! Very soon!"

The jogger frowned, "So, we're all going to die?"

"Yes, soon."

With a shrug, the jogger declared, "Well, fuck jogging then. I'm going to get a donut."

Larry, getting more frustrated with each passing moment, yells to the jogger "I don't give a shit what you do! The four horsemen are coming!"

"Hey! Watch your language; there are children present," a mother admonished.

"He just said the F-word!" Larry pointed out.

"No, I didn't!" the jogger defended.

"Yes, you did! You just said, f– jogging!" Larry countered.

"Oh, maybe I did. I'm sorry, ma'am, I should be more conscious of what I yell in the streets," the jogger admitted sheepishly.

The mother smiled, "It's okay. It's not the end of the world."

"Yes! Yes it is!" Larry screams.

The teen looked up from their smartphone to make contact with Larry once more, "Why should we listen to you? Like, who even are you?"

"My name is Larry, but you all can call me the Apocalyptic Street Preacher." Larry confidently let out.

"Yeah, no. We're not going to call you that, Larry." the teen replied.

A tourist, map in hand, inquired, "Where are the pegasus?"

Larry sighed, "They're not pegasus! They're horses! And, I don't know. They're… they're training."

"For what? The world's ending," the jogger retorted with a chuckle.

"Don't you have a donut to eat?" Larry snapped.

With the fading echoes of laughter and banter behind him, Larry descended from his soapbox, weary and defeated. He wove his way through the city streets, the weight of his message hanging heavily on his shoulders.

As he unlocked the door to his modest apartment, the faint city noises dwindled to a hushed murmur. Larry placed his well-worn Bible on a small table near the window. Sitting in the dim light, he allowed himself a moment of reflection. The city's skepticism seemed unfounded to him; he had seen signs, felt the ominous stirrings.

Gazing out of the window, a solitary star blinked in the dusky expanse. And for all the day's mockery and jests, Larry knew one undeniable truth: the riders on their flying steeds, not like Pegasus but horses, were indeed drawing near. The end of the world, whether believed or ridiculed, was imminent.

# CHAPTER 2

# THE SCROTAL SWORD

The scent of gunpowder and sweat hung in the air. The ground, uneven and muddy, was a treacherous landscape of craters and fallen soldiers. The cacophony of war raged all around — shouts of commanders, cries of the wounded, the steady percussion of gunfire. But amid the chaos, one figure stood tall, unfazed by the bullets whizzing past and the explosions threatening to engulf everything.

It was Cassian.

His jet-black hair, streaked with blood-red lines, whipped wildly in the battlefield winds, echoing the ferocity in his crimson eyes. His dark, ornate armor was an enigma of eras past, clashing starkly with the modern warfare surrounding him. Every inch of him screamed of wars fought, of countless battles — each scar telling its own story.

Soldiers, seeing Cassian's intimidating aura, initially hesitated, trying to discern which side he was on. But their hesitation cost them dearly.

With a focused, almost manic determination, Cassian charged forward. And as he ran, every soldier unfortunate enough to cross his path met the same gory fate: a swift, brutal strike to the crotch. Cassian's weapon, dripping with the gruesome evidence of his unique battle technique, was a blur as he moved from one opponent to the next.

"Is this guy for real?" gasped a young private, watching from behind a makeshift barricade. His senior officer, just as horrified, simply nodded, unable to articulate a response.

Cassian's path of destruction seemed endless. Soldier after soldier crumpled to the ground, clutching their injured regions and letting out agonized groans. It was clear he had a mission, a vendetta even, and he executed it with ruthless precision.

Amid the destruction, however, something began to shift in Cassian's demeanor. With each strike, a hint of confusion, a glimmer of introspection began to cloud his eyes. The mindless rage that propelled him seemed to waver. He paused, his fierce gaze scanning the battlefield, the countless wounded, the sheer horror of it all.

"Why...?" he whispered to himself, his voice breaking the war's mayhem, even if just for a moment.

But before he could further contemplate the nature of his actions, the ground trembled. Great doors — massive, ancient, and seemingly out of place in this war-torn scenario — appeared ahead of him. They slowly creaked open, revealing blinding light.

The familiar, shrill sound of machinery winding down filled the air, making Cassian shield his eyes. The battlefield, the noise, the injured soldiers — they all began to fade, pixelating into nothingness.

Elara, slender and graceful, stood at the console of the now evident simulator. She reached for a switch, her fingers brushing the controls with an almost caressing touch, and the entire world around Cassian went silent. The simulation was over.

Cassian, breathing heavily, looked around, disoriented. The contrast from the battlefield to the sterile, quiet room was jarring. He met Elara's eyes, a mixture of amusement and concern reflecting in her gaze.

"That was... unique," she remarked, an eyebrow raised.

Cassian, still catching his breath, simply grunted in response.

Elara, with an amused smirk playing on her lips, took a step closer to Cassian, her gaze fixed on the towering figure still trying to regain his composure. "Was that... training? Because if it was, I think you might have misunderstood the goal."

Cassian, wiping sweat from his brow, looked at her defiantly. "I was just... trying something different."

Elara chuckled, "Different? Cassian, the simulator is for training, not for... indulging in whatever twisted pleasure you get from stabbing everyone in the dick."

Cassian's face turned a shade redder, "Look, it's just... satisfying, okay?"

She laughed, her melodious voice echoing in the room, "You find stabbing people in the dick satisfying? By the gods, Cassian. That's... specific."

"It's a tactical move." Cassian defended, albeit weakly.

"Tactical? When in any historical or futuristic battle has the primary strategy been 'go for the dick'? Seriously?"

Cassian grumbled, "It catches them off guard."

Elara, clearly enjoying the playful banter, leaned in, "How many dicks did you manage to stab this time around?"

"Lost count after fifty," Cassian admitted, a hint of pride in his voice.

She shook her head, chuckling. "You're unbelievable. And while we're on the subject of training, have you seen Ezriel? Because I think the last time I saw him was... what? A hundred years ago?"

Cassian shrugged, "Probably. To be honest, I don't think any of us have been training seriously for centuries. Ezriel just stopped showing up one day, and none of us really questioned it."

Elara smirked, "Maybe he got tired of watching you repetitively stab dicks."

Cassian rolled his eyes, "Alright, alright, I get it. I'll... diversify my tactics next time."

"Please do," Elara replied, her voice dripping with mock concern. "After all, you wouldn't want to be known as the Horseman who only goes for the dick."

Cassian snorted, "There are worse titles."

The two shared a laugh, their bond evident, even amid the playful teasing.

# CHAPTER 3

# A Call to Reckoning

In a lavish and eclectic room, filled with artifacts from various eras, sat Ezriel and Liora. Ezriel was lounging on an opulent Roman chaise, munching on ancient Roman olives and humming a tune unmistakably from the 1980s. Liora, on the other hand, was meticulously organizing a shelf, dusting off artifacts and occasionally scribbling something on her modern tablet.

Just as Ezriel started to whistle the chorus to "Take On Me," a shrill ringtone broke the ambiance. He scrambled to find the ancient-looking phone amidst the piles of 19th-century candies. On answering, he tilted the phone away to ask Liora, "How do you put this on speaker again?" She sighed, pressing the button for him.

The voice on the other end was imperious. "Ezriel, how fares the training of the Four Horsemen?"

Ezriel straightened up, his relaxed demeanor replaced by one of feigned professionalism. "Ah, the Horsemen! They have been training rigorously for centuries under our watchful guidance."

Liora looked up from her tablet, her eyebrow arched in a sharp curve of disbelief.

The voice continued, "Good. Because they need to be ready in two weeks."

"Two weeks?" Ezriel choked on an olive, which Liora deftly slapped out of him. "Of course, two weeks. That will be no problem at all."

The call ended abruptly, and the weight of the situation started to sink in. Ezriel's jovial tune was replaced with a stunned silence.

Liora put down her tablet, taking a deep breath. "Ezriel," she began, her voice dripping with sarcasm, "remind me again how you've been training them for centuries?"

Ezriel looked sheepishly around the room, avoiding her piercing gaze. "Well, you know, we had that one training session... umm, a few centuries ago, and then... oh, the Renaissance happened, and things got busy..."

Liora interrupted him, "You mean you got distracted."

Ezriel fidgeted, "Maybe... a little."

Pouring a cup of tea, Liora handed it to him. "Feeling stressed, Ezriel? I have a tea for that."

Ezriel took the cup, grateful for the distraction. "We need a plan," he mumbled into his tea.

Liora nodded, her sharp eyes scanning the room. "First, we find out where they are and what they've been up to."

Ezriel looked perplexed. "You mean, you don't know?"

"I've been busy sorting our ancient tea collection," Liora replied with a straight face.

The two of them hurriedly began moving across the Academy's vast and ornate corridors, the marble floors echoing their frantic steps. The towering statues of past apocalypse averters watched them rush by with stoic indifference.

"Hang on," Liora stopped, pointing towards a smudge of what looked like tomato soup on the pristine white marble. "Someone's been having lunch on the go."

Following the drips and drops, they soon stumbled upon Elara and Cassian, still in mid-conversation by the simulator. The glowing holograms inside the simulator displayed an array of unfortunate soldiers, most of them clutching their... well, nether regions.

Ezriel sighed with relief. "Elara! Cassian! Thank the ancient deities! We need to find Morten and Seraphel and—"

Elara raised a hand, cutting him off. "Calm down, ancient one. They're probably stuffing their faces with grilled cheese in the food hall."

Ezriel blinked. "You knew where they were?"

"Well, yeah," Cassian chimed in, a smirk on his face. "We've been here for centuries."

They began sprinting down the corridors, with Ezriel muttering about their timeline. "Two weeks... two weeks... We have only two weeks..."

Between breaths, Elara explained, "By the way, Cassian hasn't been 'training'. He's just been enjoying his... unique method."

Cassian shrugged defensively. "It's cathartic."

As the group reached the grand food hall, they found Morten and Seraphel sitting at a long table.

Ezriel exhaled, "Finally! We're all together."

Elara, raised an eyebrow. "Ezriel, did you think we had left the Academy?"

Ezriel scratched his head sheepishly. "I might've... assumed. The Academy's grounds are vast, after all."

A collective gasp spread among the horsemen. Morten spoke up, "Wait, we go outside!?"

Liora clarified, "You can go outside but you can't leave the Academy grounds. Haven't you ever seen the door at the end of the food hall?"

Ezriel pointed towards a huge door at the end of the food hall. "That door leads outside. How do you think Ted and I meet to get food supplies?"

Cassian furrowed his brow, "Who the hell is Ted?"

Elara shook her head, clearly exasperated. "Never mind Ted. You're saying we could've had different food at any point?"

Ezriel looked around the hall, which boasted a massive kitchen. "You guys don't like the food options?"

"It's not that we don't like it," Cassian declared, "that's all we've eaten for nearly two thousand years!"

Morten chimed in, "I've always wondered where the crab came from."

Liora looked bewildered. "So... nobody ever tried to open that door?"

Seraphel raised her hand. "I thought Cassian did."

Cassian shrugged. "I thought Morten did."

Ezriel facepalmed. "None of you? Really?"

The Horsemen shared awkward glances.

"To be fair," Liora sighed, taking a sip from her ever-present tea cup, "We should've probably had an orientation day."

# CHAPTER 4

# HEIGHTENED URGENCY

Ezriel, with a grand flourish, climbed atop the nearest table. The ancient wood creaked under his weight, his silver hair glinting under the chandeliers.

"Why are you on the table? We're all standing right here," Seraphel pointed out, quirking an eyebrow.

Cassian smirked, "Yeah, we can hear you. Unless you're going to start dancing or something?"

Ezriel adjusted his robe, a bit embarrassed but undeterred. "Because this is important! We have a grave situation at hand!"

There was a pause, and then Morten said dryly, "You could've said that without the height advantage."

Brushing off the snide remarks, Ezriel took a deep breath. "Now, listen closely. We're going to use the simulator. Each of you will go in, one by one, and showcase your powers. Demonstrate how you'd bring about the apocalypse."

Elara looked skeptical. "A virtual doomsday? Sounds... fun?"

Ezriel pointed at her. "Elara, you're up first. Famine needs to be front and center."

Cassian snickered. "Good luck. Don't turn all the simulator characters into skinny vegans."

Elara shot him a glare but before she could retort, the horsemen began to move towards the exit. Their collective footsteps echoed in the grand hall.

Ezriel's voice, already high-pitched with stress, rose an octave. "Where do you think you're going?"

Seraphel, always the diplomat, said, "A quick walk outside? Get some fresh air?"

"We're leaving," Cassian stated plainly, pointing at the door Ezriel had shown them earlier.

Morten added, "Yeah, and maybe grab some food that isn't on the regular menu."

Ezriel jumped off the table, his robe billowing behind him, trying to block their path. "You can't leave now! We only have two weeks!"

Elara, her arms crossed, shot back, "Sounds like a you problem, not a us problem."

Liora, ever the voice of reason, interjected, "Look, let's compromise. We'll run the simulations, but maybe we can mix in some outside breaks? Variety is the spice of life, after all."

Ezriel looked like he was about to have a heart attack, but he slowly nodded. "Fine. But no more than an hour each day. We're on a tight schedule."

The horsemen exchanged glances, and after a moment, Cassian said, "Deal. But we choose the restaurants."

Ezriel's eyes widened, "Restaurants? You can't possibly mean outside the Academy!"

Morten grinned cheekily, "Well, why not? A little bit of cordon bleu, maybe some filet mignon, some—"

Ezriel raised a hand to stop him, "Enough! We have provisions here to last us two weeks. Besides, you can't just gallivant around Earth before the appointed time."

Elara pouted, "So no sushi?"

Liora shook her head, tapping on her smartwatch, "There's plenty here. We've been stocked for all kinds of scenarios. And to be honest, some of these supplies are quite gourmet."

Ezriel interjected, "Look, I get it. Two millennia of tomato soup, crab cakes, and cheese burgers can wear on anyone's palate. But we need to stay focused and remain in the Academy. Earth isn't prepared for you yet."

Seraphel looked contemplative, "You're saying that in two weeks, we can roam Earth? For real this time?"

"Yes," Ezriel replied gravely. "But only if you all abide by the training regimen and stay put."

# OF RESTRAURANTS AND RUIN

Inside the expansive realm of the simulator, Elara found herself on Earth, amidst the hustle and bustle of human society. She could see the energy of human life, the laughter, conversations, and above all, their relentless consumption of food.

First, she dashed into a bustling restaurant, gleefully throwing plates of spaghetti, salads, and steaks onto the floor. People screamed, some jumped out of their seats, and many took out their phones to record the chaos.

Exiting the restaurant with a proud smirk on her face, she glanced over and saw another eatery just across the street. As she started to make her way over, the simulation suddenly paused.

The lively street scene became like a frozen tableau, and Ezriel appeared beside her. "Elara," he said, shaking his head with exasperation, "You can't just run from restaurant to restaurant tossing out dinners. That won't cause a worldwide famine."

Elara scoffed, "It's a start."

The scene morphed, and they were now in the middle of a sprawling farmland. Without missing a beat, Elara sprinted through fields, trampling lettuce heads, tearing out carrots, and squishing tomatoes underfoot. She felt triumphant, but that victory was short-lived as the scene froze once again.

"Ezriel!" Elara exclaimed in frustration.

"That," Ezriel said pointedly, "is just one farm. Ruining a single farm's produce isn't going to lead to famine."

Elara rolled her eyes but nodded. "Alright, alright, give me another shot."

Suddenly, the scene changed again. The familiar sliding doors of a grocery store greeted her. Determined, Elara entered, her eyes scanning the aisles. Hours seemed to go by as she moved with purpose, and by the time she exited, it was nighttime in the simulation.

Ezriel was leaning against a lamppost, checking a simulated wristwatch that didn't really exist. "Well? What did you do this time?"

Elara grinned triumphantly, "I got rid of all the condiments."

Ezriel looked at her in disbelief. "You... what?"

She shrugged, "Think about it. No ketchup for fries, no mayonnaise for sandwiches, no mustard for hotdogs. People will refuse to eat their bland food!"

Ezriel couldn't help but chuckle. "That's... an interesting strategy. But I doubt it will cause an apocalypse."

"They won't just be missing out on flavor," Elara continued, "Condiments often act as preservatives. Without them, food will spoil faster."

Ezriel paused, contemplating her reasoning. "You have a point. But we can't rely on that alone. And we don't have the luxury of time to see if it would work."

Elara sighed, "Fine, back to the drawing board then."

"We'll come up with another strategy," Ezriel said, placing a reassuring hand on her shoulder. "But for now, let's regroup with the others."

Ezriel and Elara re-entered the common area to find Liora, Cassian, Morten, and Seraphel chatting. Cassian looked up, a smirk on his face, "So, how did it go?"

Elara rolled her eyes, "It's a work in progress."

Morten chuckled, "Sounds like you had fun."

Ezriel cleared his throat, regaining control of the situation. "We don't have the luxury of time. Seraphel, you're up next."

Seraphel rose gracefully from her seat, her regal posture evident. Her white armor caught the light in a way that made it seem like she was glowing. "Very well," she said, her voice commanding yet melodic.

# Division

# Dilemmas

As Seraphel observed the simulated Earth, she witnessed a scene that defied her expectations. Everywhere she looked, people greeted each other warmly, exchanging pleasantries and laughing at shared jokes. There wasn't a hint of division.

"This is Earth?" Seraphel asked incredulously.

Ezriel nodded, "This is an exact simulation of Earth. It was created centuries ago to replicate the expected advancement of the human species."

"They're so unified," she observed.

Ezriel's voice was filled with a mixture of admiration and regret, "Humanity has had its challenges—medieval times, the Spanish Crusades, even the death of Harambe—but through it all, they've grown stronger, more unified, and more connected."

Seraphel took a deep breath, steeling herself. "And my job, as the horseman of conquest, is to divide and conquer."

Ezriel gave a grave nod. "Exactly."

*Attempt 1: The Sports Showdown*

Her first strategy was simple. She introduced a grand sporting event: "The Unity Cup," pitting two teams against one another. Surely, such a competitive event would lead to disagreements, heated arguments, and divisions?

But as the games concluded, something unexpected occurred. No matter how fierce the competition, the teams embraced each other, laughing and celebrating the spirit of the game. Fans from both sides cheered together, raising toasts to impressive plays, irrespective of the team that made them.

Ezriel, observing from the side, chuckled. "Seems like the spirit of sportsmanship is stronger here."

*Attempt 2: Feast or Famine*

Next, Seraphel decided to tap into culinary passions. She introduced a variety of exotic foods, hoping to create a divide between different dietary preferences. But instead of heated debates about the superiority of dishes, it turned into a massive food festival. People excitedly sampled dishes from other cultures, swapping recipes and stories.

"Ah, the universal language of food," Ezriel commented, slightly amused.

*Attempt 3: Fashion Faux Pas*

With a snap of her fingers, Seraphel introduced bizarre fashion trends, expecting to create rifts between fashion elites and others. But the streets became a riot of color and fun as people paraded around in outlandish outfits, complimenting each other's unique tastes.

Ezriel shook his head, grinning. "Now that's a look."

*Attempt 4: The Pet Parade*

Thinking that perhaps age-old arguments about pets might do the trick, Seraphel pitted cats against dogs. To her astonishment, instead of the expected division, there was a jovial parade where cats sat atop dogs, and humans celebrated their shared love for animals.

"You're really batting a thousand here," Ezriel said, his laughter echoing.

*Attempt 5: The Melody of Unity*

Seraphel introduced a variety of music genres, hoping to ignite a musical war of sorts. But to her bewilderment, it led to a grand concert of harmonious blended genres. People of all ages danced together, celebrating the rhythm of unity.

Ezriel hummed along. "Quite the catchy tune, this unity."


*Attempt 6: Lost and Connected*

Scattering valuable items everywhere, Seraphel waited for the disputes to begin. But instead, she witnessed a series of heartwarming moments where items were returned, and friendships were forged.

Ezriel smirked, "Guess they value connections over possessions."


*Attempt 7: Rumor Rundown*

Finally, in a desperate bid, Seraphel started a harmless rumor, hoping it would spiral into a web of misunderstandings. Yet, once again, the simulated humans sought direct communication, clarifying any misconceptions and laughing over the absurdities.

Ezriel approached Seraphel, placing a comforting hand on her shoulder. "You tried. It seems this world's unity isn't so easily disrupted."

Seraphel sighed, feeling both frustrated and in awe of the harmony she'd witnessed. "Perhaps the real lesson here is to understand such unity before attempting to divide it."

Ezriel nodded, "Indeed. Every challenge brings wisdom. Let's see how Cassian fares."


As they exited the simulation, Seraphel couldn't help but wonder if, in their quest for division, they might discover something even more profound.

# CHAPTER 7

# THE ART OF WAR

The simulator hummed to life, its greenish glow enveloping the room. Cassian found himself in the lavish office of a president of an unnamed country. The high-backed leather chair, the mahogany desk, and the walls lined with bookshelves and accolades created an ambiance of power.

However, the most intriguing object was the decorative sword mounted above the doorway. Without hesitation, Cassian lunged for it, unsheathing the blade with practiced ease. In a flurry of motion, he began his rampage, targeting every unsuspecting victim in a most... unconventional manner.

Ezriel's voice boomed, causing the simulation to halt mid-action. "Cassian! Stop!"

The room returned to its normal state, and Cassian stood there, the decorative sword still in his hand, looking both surprised and slightly disappointed.

"You can't just stab everyone in the dick," Ezriel reprimanded, his tone filled with frustration.

Cassian blinked innocently. "Why not?"

"That won't cause the end of times, Cassian."

Cassian swung the sword with flair, "But, I'm really good at it! Like fifty dicks an hour!"

Ezriel sighed, rubbing his temples. "No, Cassian. You have to learn to create war, not fight in it. And besides, stabbing everyone like that... it's just not cool, man."

Cassian's shoulders slumped. "Fine. What do you suggest then?".

Ezriel's voice held a weight of gravitas. "Wars in this age aren't just about battles. They're about information, manipulation, and vulnerability. You need to sow discord, mistrust. You need to be the spark in the powder keg."

Absorbing the weight of Ezriel's words, Cassian took a deep breath, focusing on his surroundings. His ears pricked at the muffled voices outside the president's door. Whispers of an imminent meeting drifted into the room, and Cassian, ever the strategist, swiftly hid himself within the room's expansive closet.

The doors swung open, and a group of men in sharp suits, along with military officials, entered the room. The president, a stern-looking figure, sat at the head of the table. Conversations about military operations, covert missions, international alliances, and trade agreements filled the room.

As the discussions grew heated, Cassian, from his hiding spot, began discreetly recording the conversation using a device he found in the president's coat pocket. Information about vulnerabilities in the defense system, internal conflicts, and even blackmail material about various global leaders were all discussed openly.

After what felt like hours, the meeting concluded. The officials left, and the room once again fell silent. Cassian emerged from his hiding spot, a satisfied smirk on his face.

Reentering the simulator's default mode, Ezriel looked impressed. "You've collected a treasure trove of information. Those secrets, if leaked, could start wars, break alliances, and bring down empires."

Cassian's eyes gleamed with a mischievous glint. "Oh, I can do chaos. Just watch."

Ezriel sighed, raking a hand through his hair. "Cassian, while your... particular penchant for stabbing has its charm, we need to think bigger. Larger scale."

Cassian cocked his head, curiosity evident. "You mean no more dicks?"

Ezriel shot him a pointed look. "No, Cassian. That's not the point. Remember, we're not here to simply cause chaos. We're here to herald the apocalypse. There's a difference."

Cassian frowned. "Explain."

"The apocalypse is about restructuring, rebalancing, forcing evolution and change," Ezriel began, his voice carrying the weight of millennia of knowledge. "Merely killing or hurting isn't the objective. You are War. You need to incite conflict on a grand scale, not just cause pain to individuals. We want nations to turn on each other, not just men clutching their groins in agony."

Cassian, still not entirely convinced, responded, "But surely there's room for a little... personal touch?"

Ezriel sighed again, softer this time. "Cassian, there's a finesse to what we do. And yes, your personal touch can be there, but it must be strategic, planned, a part of the bigger picture. If you're going to stab, let it be metaphorical. Stab at their pride, their trust, their relationships. The information you gathered? Use it. Leverage it. Make them distrust each other."

Cassian took a moment to let the words sink in, his brow furrowed in thought. Then, slowly, a wicked grin spread across his face. "Alright, fine. No more literal stabbing. But I promise you, Ezriel, the world will feel the blade of War's influence."

Ezriel nodded, satisfied. "That's all I ask. Now, go get Morten. He's next."

# CHAPTER 8

# MORTEN'S RESURRECTION MISSTEPS

As the simulator hummed to life, Morten was instantly surrounded by a dense, ethereal fog, signaling his arrival in the realm of the departed. Souls floated around like wraiths, and though many were unfamiliar and potentially terrifying figures of the past, Morten's steps seemed to have a distinct direction.

Ezriel observed from a distance, hopeful to see the harbinger of death select the most menacing souls to bring about destruction. But as Morten waved his hand, the first figure to solidify was... a librarian. Mild-mannered, slightly balding, and holding a stack of overdue books, Gilbert, the librarian from Morten's childhood, looked around in astonishment.

Ezriel's eyes widened in disbelief. "Morten! Of all the souls, you chose... him?"

But before he could get a response, Morten was off again, deeper into the mist. This time he stopped near a soul wearing a hard hat, carrying a lunchbox. The figure materialized as Bob, the friendly construction worker from down the street of Morten's past life, who always greeted him with a wave.

"Now, wait just a min—" Ezriel began, but Morten, seemingly on a mission, was already making his third choice.

And then, bounding joyfully towards them was not a person at all, but a dog. A golden retriever, to be exact, wagging its tail, seemingly excited to be back. Morten knelt down, hugging the dog. "Oh, Mr. Whiskers! How I've missed you!"

Ezriel, hands on his hips, finally had enough. "Morten! What are you doing? We need warriors, leaders, titans of industry! Not... librarians, construction workers, and dogs!"

Morten, still clutching Mr. Whiskers, looked up sheepishly. "I... I just wanted to be with familiar souls. Ones that wouldn't scare me."

Ezriel sighed, "Morten, you're the embodiment of Death. You shouldn't be... skittish."

Morten looked down, "I've always been this way. Even as Death, I've found solace in the familiar, the comforting. I thought... maybe my friends could help?"

Ezriel softened his gaze, realizing that even among the mighty Horsemen, vulnerabilities existed. "Alright. But we need to figure out a way to channel your power towards our goal."

Morten nodded, releasing Mr. Whiskers who happily bounded off into the simulated park. "I'll try harder. I promise."

Just as the words left Morten's mouth, a strange pallor came over him. His usually pale complexion turned even whiter, like a sheet of paper. His knees buckled, and before anyone could react, he collapsed onto the ground.

Ezriel rushed to his side, trying to gauge his friend's condition. "Morten! Speak to me!"

Morten's eyes fluttered open weakly, his voice barely above a whisper. "I'm... so hungry."

Ezriel frowned. "Hungry? Why haven't you eaten?"

Morten managed a weak smile, "There's no ketchup."

The statement seemed so ludicrous that Ezriel was momentarily speechless. He was about to retort when the simulator's doors swished open to reveal Elara, a triumphant grin on her face.

"It worked!" she announced proudly.

Ezriel turned to her, his frustration evident. "Did you take the ketchup?"

"Yup," Elara replied nonchalantly.

Morten's voice, though weak, held a touch of indignation. "You try eating a cheeseburger without ketchup!? I'd rather die!"

Ezriel tried to bring the conversation back to a logical point. "Why didn't you eat the grilled cheese and tomato soup?"

Morten scowled, "I've been eating grilled cheese and tomato soup for two thousand years! I can't do it again! You ruined my favorite comfort food!"

"And the crab cakes?" Ezriel continued, trying to understand Morten's unique dietary restrictions.

Morten's face twisted in disgust, "I have never and will never touch those crab cakes! I don't see an ocean around here, do you?"

Elara, thoroughly enjoying herself, chimed in with a smirk, "I told you it would work."

Ezriel let out an exasperated sigh. Between Morten's fainting spells over ketchup and Elara's mischievous games, he realized that bringing about the apocalypse might be more challenging than he originally thought.

# CHAPTER 9

# Elara's
# Awakening

In the dim glow of the simulator room, Ezriel set the coordinates for their a new trial. Elara stood poised, the weight of her mission evident in her focused gaze. As the scene materialized, they found themselves amidst a neighborhood barbecue, filled with the cheerful cacophony of laughter, sizzling meats, and children playing.

Without a word, Elara quickly moved to the barbecue stations, removing propane tanks. The joyous atmosphere became tinged with confusion as grills went cold and meats remained uncooked.

Ezriel, not entirely impressed, waved his hand, resetting the scene. "We're aiming for famine, Elara. Not an inconvenient barbecue."

The atmosphere morphed, replacing suburban homes with rows of crops stretching to the horizon. Elara, understanding the hint, went straight for the farm's irrigation system. Swiftly, she sabotaged the lifeline of the crops. It was a better attempt, yet still localized.

"We're getting closer," Ezriel encouraged. "But famine isn't just about food. It's about the scarcity of resources."

The simulator's familiar hum signaled the transition, and soon, the vibrant mountain landscape surrounded Elara and Ezriel. The mighty rush of the river provided a constant backdrop, its waters an artery of life for the valleys below.

Elara, dressed in earthy tones, stood at the riverbank, taking in the vastness of the terrain. Ezriel appeared beside her, his eyes scanning the surroundings. "Water is life," he began, "If you can control it, famine will surely follow."

Elara nodded, her gaze fixed on the river. "Without water, crops wither, animals perish, and civilizations crumble," she murmured.

The simulator's familiar hum signaled the transition, and soon, the vibrant mountain landscape surrounded Elara and Ezriel. The mighty rush of the river provided a constant backdrop, its waters an artery of life for the valleys below.

Ezriel, ever the strategist, pointed upstream. "Water has always been a symbol of life. Halt its journey, and famine is inevitable."

Elara, feeling an almost magnetic pull towards the river, responded, "And yet, it's not just about stopping the flow. It's about understanding it, feeling its essence."

Ezriel observed her curiously. "You've always had a unique connection to the elements."

She approached the narrower section of the river, her fingers skimming the surface. The water responded to her touch, rippling outwards in concentric circles. Although it was a subtle reaction, it was clear that Elara had an affinity with the element.

Spotting a cluster of large boulders on the mountainside and trees with precarious roots, an idea began to form. Drawing upon her deep connection with the environment, she felt the weight and balance of each stone, the strength of the tree roots, and the flow of the river.

Using tools she fashioned from the environment and guided by her innate understanding, she began her work. She positioned the boulders and felled trees in strategic locations, creating a natural dam. As she worked, there were moments when it seemed like the earth was aiding her, with rocks fitting perfectly and trees falling just right.

The dam took form, and the river's mighty rush began to slow, creating a serene lake upstream while reducing the flow downstream to a mere trickle.

Ezriel watched the newly formed lake shimmer in the simulated sunlight, the ripples casting fleeting, silvery patterns upon its surface. He turned to Elara, admiration evident in his gaze. "You've not only halted the river, but you've shown a profound understanding of balance. It's impressive."

Elara's cheeks tinted a soft rose at the praise, but she waved it off modestly. "It's just about listening, really. The world speaks; we just need to tune in."

Ezriel clapped her on the shoulder, his demeanor softened by pride. "That was impressive, Elara. Truly. But now, it's Seraphel's turn."

She nodded, catching her breath. "Of course. I'll fetch her."

Ezriel watched as Elara walked away, the glint of accomplishment still evident in her stride. The simulator, with all its infinite potentials and scenarios, was proving to be an invaluable tool in harnessing the Horsemen's powers. But more than that, it was becoming a crucible, revealing facets of their personalities and abilities they hadn't previously recognized.

# CHAPTER 10
# CONQUEST AND COMPROMISE

The simulation room's door slid open with a hiss, revealing Seraphel's statuesque form. Ezriel, expecting to instruct her on the upcoming simulation, looked up in mild surprise. She had an air of confidence, almost as if she didn't need any further training.

"No need for simulations, Ezriel," Seraphel said with a smirk, her voice echoing slightly in the cavernous chamber.

Ezriel raised an eyebrow, intrigued. "Oh? Why's that?"

Seraphel gestured for him to follow. "Come, let me show you."

Ezriel followed her through the labyrinthine corridors of their base until they reached the expansive food hall. The scene that unfolded before them was both comical and concerning.

Morten and Cassian lay on opposite ends of the room, a clear chalk line drawn down the center. While Morten clutched at his crotch, grimacing in pain, Cassian was curled into a tight ball, his usually fierce demeanor replaced with one of sheer terror.

Ezriel stared at the tableau, his expression a mix of confusion and exasperation. "What off earth happened here?"

Seraphel chuckled, "I thought it would be fun to initiate a game of territories. Gave Morten one side and Cassian the other. Seemed harmless enough."

Ezriel glanced at the distribution. On Morten's side were the stacks of food and beverages, while on Cassian's side lay the entrance to the restrooms.

A groan from Morten broke the brief silence, "It was all fun and games until I realized I couldn't get to the restroom without crossing Cassian's territory."

"And I," Cassian managed to say, "hadn't eaten in hours! But the food was on his side."

Seraphel shrugged, a hint of mischief in her eyes. "It began as a mere agreement. Trade access for food or restroom. But things escalated. Dramatically."

Morten interjected, "He kicked me! Right in the—"

"We get the picture," Ezriel said, holding up a hand.

"And then," Cassian whispered, pointing to a specter floating near the corner, "he brought him."

Ezriel's gaze followed Cassian's shaky finger to see the unmistakable figure of Bob Marley, strumming his guitar and singing "One Love."

"Bob Marley? Really, Morten?"

Morten shrugged defensively, "He's an embodiment of peace. Cassian is War. I thought it'd calm things down."

Cassian whimpered, "It's... it's too much peace. It's overwhelming."

Suddenly, a cheerful voice chimed in, "Oh, Bob's just the best! You should try his tea!" Turning around, Ezriel spotted Liora swaying gently next to Marley, clearly in a delightful haze.

Ezriel sighed, pinching the bridge of his nose. "Alright. We need to sort this out." He looked at Seraphel, "I assume this was your version of conquest?"

Seraphel nodded, her eyes gleaming with mischief and pride. "Exactly. But not in the way you might think. Instead of trying to conquer others, my strategy is to cultivate an environment where they feel the compulsion to conquer one another."

Ezriel paused, letting the words sink in. He observed Morten and Cassian, still in their respective states of discomfort and fear. He then looked at Bob Marley and Liora, serenading the room with their harmonious vocals. The whole scenario was a perfect display of Seraphel's newfound tactic.

"I must say," Ezriel began, a hint of admiration in his voice, "this is rather ingenious. Instead of expending energy and resources trying to control every individual, you've essentially turned them on each other. It's an internal collapse."

Seraphel smiled, pleased. "Exactly. It's the kind of chaos that feeds on itself. Once set into motion, it becomes self-perpetuating. It requires little to no intervention from us, making our job much easier."

Ezriel chuckled, "Indeed. It's a more refined and cunning approach to conquest. Using psychology and the natural desires and fears of individuals to set them against one another. I must admit, I'm impressed."

Seraphel inclined her head in acknowledgment. "Thank you. I thought it would be a fitting adaptation for the modern age."

The two stood in contemplation for a moment, watching the scene unfold before them, reflecting on the evolving nature of the apocalypse and the methods they'd employ to bring it about.

# CHAPTER 11

# ECHOES
# OF LIFE

The simulator buzzed to life, the ambient lighting instantly shifting from the sterile white of the training room to the soft, somber illumination of a bygone era. Morten found himself in a quaint, rustic chamber. An elderly woman, her face lined with the tales of countless memories, lay motionless on an ancient wooden bed. The hushed atmosphere was only broken by the soft whimpers of an unusual dog, its coat a striking mix of white and gold, nudging the woman's limp hand with a mournful sigh.

A pang of urgency surged within Morten. Desperation clawed at him, urging him to act. He tried to administer CPR, pushing down on her chest in hopes of rekindling the spark of life within her. But despite his fervent efforts, the finality of death began to settle, and the room plunged into a silence that weighed heavily on his soul.

The room's silence was broken by Morten's heart-wrenching cry. "What's the lesson here, Ezriel? Why?"

Ezriel's voice, usually calm and measured, held a hint of sadness. "Morten, these modules aren't my creation. They are set to challenge and reveal."

Desperation seeped into Morten's voice. "Rewind it, Ezriel. Please!"

In their frantic struggle to gain control, the rewind button was pressed down, jamming it.

Time began to move backward, painting the tapestry of the woman's life in reverse strokes.

From the outer edges of the simulation, the woman's days as a revered healer emerged. With every town and village she visited, people looked at her with a mix of respect and awe. Everywhere she went, she spread wisdom and inspiration.  In her wake, she left communities transformed, filled with hope and a deeper understanding of spiritual teachings. Always by her side was the dog, a silent witness to all her acts of kindness and compassion.

As they traveled further back, a serene setting materialized, revealing the tranquil grounds of a Buddhist monastery. There, she spent countless hours, days even, in deep meditation. The tranquility of the setting and the depth of her practice spoke of years of refuge, a sanctuary from a world that had perhaps dealt her harsh blows.

And then, the bustling streets of a city appeared, where amidst the noise and chaos, the woman's figure stood out. Her once radiant eyes now held shadows of despair, portraying a deep-rooted sorrow. She wandered the streets aimlessly, lost in delusion and denial, a stark contrast to the beacon of hope she would later become. The poignant sight of her being largely ignored, regarded as just another homeless soul by the rushing crowds, was heart-wrenching.

A smoky haze next enveloped the scene, bringing forth the most painful memory. The charred remains of what was once a dwelling stood stark against the backdrop of night, the flames having consumed not just her home but also her beloved poet husband. The weight of this tragic event, the fulcrum upon which her life had pivoted, was palpable.

The scene transformed once again, this time to brighter days, where young love and passion reigned supreme. She was surrounded by family, by joy, and by the beautiful verses of her poet love. The world seemed full of possibilities, their days filled with the cadence of poetry and the colors of art.

As the simulation continued its rewind, the woman regressed from a spirited child to an infant and then to a delicate unborn baby, floating serenely in a translucent sphere. The scene was one of pure serenity, a glimpse into the beginnings of life. However, this too began to fade as the baby, ever so slowly, reduced in size, becoming a mere speck and then finally vanishing into nothingness.

Morten, deeply affected by what he had witnessed, stared at the now empty space. "The impermanence of it all," he murmured, his voice choked with emotion. "It's not just about the end. Throughout her journey, there were so many moments, so many phases. All transient. All fleeting."

Ezriel nodded, contemplating Morten's words. "It's a profound realization, isn't it? That impermanence isn't just about the eventual cessation of life but about every moment, every phase. It might be the very essence of existence itself."

Morten looked up, his eyes clouded with doubt. "But what does it mean for me? For my role in the apocalypse? How do I bring about 'death' when life itself is a series of deaths and rebirths?"

Ezriel placed a reassuring hand on Morten's shoulder. "I wish I had all the answers for you, Morten. But perhaps it's not about understanding every facet now. When the time comes, I believe you will know. Your intuition, your very essence, will guide you."

Morten took a deep breath, attempting to find solace in Ezriel's words. They both knew the weight of the impending apocalypse was immense, but with understanding and introspection, they hoped to find clarity in their roles and purpose.

# CHAPTER 12

# THE BATTLE OF OPPOSITES

The simulator hummed to life, surrounding Cassian in a world both familiar yet strange. It resembled a battlefield, but the usual sounds of clashing swords and battle cries were absent. Instead, silence reigned, broken only by the footsteps of his approaching opponent: Anti-Cassian.

They began to circle each other warily, eyes locked. Every twitch, every subtle shift was mirrored by the other, though in an exaggerated, opposite manner.

Cassian tried a straightforward approach first. With a quick dart to his right, he expected to close the distance between them. But Anti-Cassian mirrored the move with an exaggerated step, maintaining the gap. Cassian scowled, slightly frustrated.

Experimenting, Cassian launched into a series of maneuvers, from high jumps to dramatic rolls. Each move was matched by Anti-Cassian with an opposite action. When Cassian leaped, Anti-Cassian ducked. When Cassian roared, Anti-Cassian whispered soothingly.

The peak of this bizarre confrontation came when Cassian, summoning his inner warrior, tried his signature low stab, targeting Anti-Cassian's... vulnerability. Instead of defending, Anti-Cassian responded by opening his arms and moving forward, attempting to pull Cassian into a hug. Cassian hesitated, then jumped back, eyebrows raised in disbelief.

"What in the seven hells...?" Cassian muttered, scratching his head.

Anti-Cassian simply smiled, his demeanor calm.

As they continued this strange dance, Cassian grew more desperate to outwit his mirror image. Hoping to trick Anti-Cassian, he approached with an open-arm hug. Anti-Cassian, in response, aimed a jab at Cassian, who chuckled. "I got you," before jumping away from the low blow.

As their duel persisted, the movements began to wane in intensity. From fierce confrontations, they morphed into gentle, synchronized steps. It felt less like a battle and more like a harmonious dance.

Amidst the synchronization, Cassian grasped the metaphorical significance: the external mayhem mirrored his internal chaos, the tussle between his impulsive side and his rational one—an eternal battle within.

The vibrant simulation faded to the stark white of the simulator room. As Cassian caught his breath, Ezriel entered, a knowing glint in his eyes. "Quite the revelation, wasn't it?"

Cassian pondered, "Today, I confronted not an enemy, but myself. The war within is profound, perhaps even more than external battles."

Ezriel settled beside him. "The mightiest warriors recognize this. Real battles rage within our minds and hearts, where hope wrestles with despair."

Absorbing this, Cassian asked, "In the apocalypse's scope, where does this internal strife fit?"

Ezriel responded with a twinkle, "Wars aren't solely on fields with swords and shields. They simmer within our souls. Harness this chaos internally, and the external world easily succumbs."

Cassian raised an eyebrow, "So, our goal isn't merely humanity's destruction?"

"No, no," Ezriel reassured with a smirk, "That's a delightful bonus. And causing internal pandemonium weakens their defenses. They become their own enemies, making our task simpler."

"Divide and conquer from within," Cassian mused.

Ezriel nodded, "Precisely. The most cataclysmic wars aren't just physical. They're psychological and emotional."

As Cassian absorbed this newfound knowledge, Ezriel playfully nudged him. "Reflect on this later. For now, assemble everyone. There's a surprise in the food hall."

Cassian, ever curious, grinned. "A surprise? For us?"

"Just ensure everyone's present," Ezriel winked, leaving Cassian in anticipation.

# A FEAST OF
# IRONY

The Academy's food hall was a grand space, walls shimmering with an otherworldly sheen. A long table stretched across the middle, set with a variety of dishes hidden under polished silver cloches, exuding an air of mystery and expectation.

Elara, Cassian, Morten, and Seraphel exchanged hopeful glances. The centuries of monotony with their meals had left them with an everlasting craving for something – anything – different.

The aroma of freshly cooked food wafted through the room, creating an ambience of anticipation. They could barely contain their excitement.

Just then, with his usual dramatic flair, Ezriel leapt onto the table. The four exchanged amused glances. "You really don't have to stand on the table, you know," Seraphel teased, "We're literally right here."

Morten chuckled, "Yeah, and it's not like we're going to listen any better just because you're a few feet higher."

Ezriel, not one to be thrown off by their teasing, cleared his throat, his robe flowing majestically around him. "Horsemen!" he began, with a tone that was meant to command attention. "Tomorrow is a big day, a day that has been centuries in the making. I know it's been... challenging, especially when it comes to our culinary limitations." He rolled his eyes for effect, causing a round of giggles. "But tonight, before our greatest mission, I wanted to give you all a taste of something different."

Elara whispered to Cassian, "If it's another version of grilled cheese, I might just bring about the apocalypse early."

Cassian tried to stifle a laugh as Ezriel continued, "Feast your eyes and satisfy your taste buds with a meal that breaks away from our usual."

With bated breath, they each reached out to the dish in front of them, lifting the ornate cover. The gasps were almost simultaneous.

"Tomato bisque and... french bread?" Elara questioned, her voice dripping with incredulity.

"Fishsticks? Seriously?" Cassian exclaimed, poking at the golden sticks with disdain.

"And... chicken patties," Morten remarked, his expression one of disbelief.

Seraphel's usually calm demeanor faltered as she stared at her plate. "Ezriel... Is this some sort of cruel joke?"

Ezriel, who seemed to anticipate joy and gratitude, was taken aback. "I thought... I mean, they're different, right?"

Cassian sighed dramatically, "Two millennia, Ezriel. Two millennia and you give us upscale versions of our usual?"

Elara added, with a smirk, "Though, I have to admit, french bread is a nice touch."

Morten, typically the calmest among them, looked at his plate and then back at Ezriel, his eyes narrowing. "They're not even upscaled versions, Ezriel. What is with you and these foods?"

Ezriel, visibly flustered, responded, "My friends Ted helped my choose them. We thought you'd like them. They're... familiar."

Cassian leaned in, trying to ease the tension, "Well, they do say 'stick to what you know.'"

But Morten was having none of it. "Ezriel," he began, his voice rising, "Where's the salad? Ever heard of it? Fresh greens, vinaigrettes, perhaps a sprinkle of feta? Or how about a juicy steak, seared to perfection, dripping with flavors of rosemary and garlic? Maybe even a risotto, creamy and rich, topped with sautéed mushrooms or fresh seafood? And don't even get me started on desserts! Tiramisu, panna cotta, crème brûlée!"

Ezriel's eyes widened with every dish Morten listed. "I... I genuinely thought this would be a pleasant surprise."

Seraphel sighed, shaking her head with mock disappointment. "You thought wrong."

Liora placed a comforting hand on Ezriel's shoulder. "It's okay, Ez. I'm sure they appreciate the effort. It's just...maybe next time consult someone other than Ted."

Morten, failing to control his rage, exclaimed, "No. We do not appreciate the effort!"

With a smirk, Cassian quipped, "Whatever. I don't care. But these fish sticks and chicken patties are going in the french bread."

Seraphel rummaged through the refrigerator, "Does anyone know where the ketchup is?"

Ezriel, trying to inject some optimism into the situation, said, "Cheer up, everyone. By this time tomorrow, you'll be on Earth, eating whatever you desire while unleashing havoc on humanity."

The room fell into a brief silence, the gravity of their impending mission momentarily sinking in. However, it didn't take long before the banter picked up where it left off.

Seraphel, holding up a fishstick, quipped, "Do you think this is what humanity eats?"

Elara chuckled, "Well, if it is, maybe we're doing them a favor."

Ezriel, sensing the futility of his efforts, sunk back into his chair, frustration evident on his face. Liora, ever calm and collected with her cup of tea in hand, leaned in, "Do you think they're ready?"

Ezriel hesitated for a moment before replying, "No, but what choice do we have?"

# CHAPTER 14

# Of Horseman and Horses

The morning sun bathed the stables in a warm golden light, casting long shadows on the ground. Four majestic steeds, each reflecting the unique personality of its designated rider, stood ready for the mission ahead.

Ezriel, hiding his nerves, stood confidently beside Liora, who was busy flipping through an ancient-looking leather-bound book, possibly a checklist of sorts. Every once in a while, she'd nod at some item or scribble a quick note.

As the four horsemen gathered, Cassian stepped forward, clearing his throat. The others exchanged curious glances, wondering what words of wisdom he would bestow upon them.

"Friends!" Cassian began, his voice echoing in the still morning air. "We have waited millennia for this day, and it's finally here! Throughout our endless waiting, I've come to know each and every one of you. And I must say, it's been quite the experience."

Elara smirked, leaning over to whisper to Seraphel, "This should be good."

Cassian continued, blissfully unaware, "Elara, with your fiery spirit and that... unique ability to turn any situation into an argument. It's been... illuminating."

Elara's eyebrows shot up in mock indignation, "Why, thank you, Cassian. I always aim to be 'illuminating.'"

Morten tried to hold back a chuckle as Cassian turned to him, "And Morten! Always so calm and level-headed. Except when you're not. Like that time with the soup incident. Never seen someone so mad at a bowl before."

Morten grimaced, remembering the ill-fated day. "It was cold, Cassian. Cold!"

Seraphel braced herself, sensing her turn was imminent. "Ah, Seraphel. Always lost in thought, often making us wonder if you're even present. But when you speak, it's... usually interesting."

She responded with a wry smile, "Thank you for your... astute observations."

Ezriel and Liora exchanged amused glances, watching as Cassian, in his misguided attempt at gratitude.

Taking a deep breath, Cassian concluded, "All I'm saying is, I couldn't have asked for a better, or more... diverse company while waiting for the apocalypse."

Ezriel, sensing the need to redirect the momentum, took a step forward. "Thank you, Cassian, for those... heartfelt words. As we prepare to send you on this important mission, remember the balance you bring to humanity and the universe."

As the four horsemen mounted their steeds, ready to gallop into their destiny, a confused look spread across Seraphel's face. "Uh, guys? How do you make it go?"

Elara looked equally puzzled, "You mean you don't know either?"

Cassian, attempting to hide his own uncertainty, tried pulling on the reins, only to be met with a disgruntled snort from his steed. "Uh, Morten?"

Morten shook his head, "I thought you'd know!"

Ezriel, his face turning several shades of red, exclaimed, "What!? But you're horsemen!"

Liora, sipping her ever-present tea, simply commented, "This is going to be a long apocalypse."

# CHAPTER 15

# APOCALYPSE, NOW IN STYLE

The morning tension still hung heavy in the air, made even thicker by the revelation that the Horsemen, destined to bring the apocalypse on horseback, had never learned to ride horses. Ezriel's face was a canvas of disbelief and exasperation.

Liora, seemingly undisturbed, set her teacup down. "Well, it seems we'll need an alternative."

Ezriel sighed, his shoulders dropping in resignation. "I had planned to give these to you after you'd successfully completed your mission. However, it appears that necessity has moved up the timeline."

With a wave of his hand, he opened a portal beside the stable. What emerged were not horses but four state-of-the-art, futuristic vehicles.

Elara, Morten, Cassian, and Seraphel stared in awe at the spectacle before them. Each car was a mechanical marvel, aesthetically designed to embody the essence of its intended driver.

Morten's car was sleek, painted a shade so dark that it seemed to absorb light. It was a machine that whispered the chilling elegance of Death.

Cassian's vehicle looked like it was forged from conflict itself—bulky, armored, and blood-red, its very form seemed to roar with the chaos of War.

Elara's car sparkled in a muted silver hue, its design minimalist yet strangely captivating. Its interiors seemed almost hollow, creating a void that felt perpetually unsatisfied.

And then there was Seraphel's. A radiant gold color covered its streamlined shape, and its interface inside appeared to be brimming with an array of controls designed for someone who would accept nothing less than total Conquest.

For a moment, everyone forgot about their minor fiasco with the horses. Cassian broke the silence, "Well, this is certainly an upgrade! Who needs horses when you can drive into the apocalypse in style?"

Ezriel composed himself and took back control of the narrative. "Each vehicle has been designed to aid you in your tasks. They are fitted with the latest apocalyptic technology. Do try to bring them back in one piece."

Elara grinned as she ran her hand over her new vehicle. "Never thought the apocalypse would be this luxurious."

Morten, already inspecting the dark interior of his car, nodded. "This should make things... efficient."

Seraphel, her eyes scanning her array of advanced controls, mused, "Finally, technology worthy of the task at hand."

Liora picked up her tea, her eyes meeting Ezriel's. "It seems the apocalypse will not just be the end, but also a new beginning, in more ways than one."

Ezriel sighed, watching as the Horsemen climbed into their respective vehicles, each eager to test its capabilities. "Indeed, Liora. Let's just hope they don't forget their purpose amidst all this... luxury."

As the roar of the engines filled the air, it quickly became evident that, just like riding, driving was not on the list of the Horsemen's skill set either.

Cassian, with an enthusiasm that seemed to surpass understanding, pushed his car into its maximum capabilities, sending it zooming across the sky like a comet. Elara's car made a series of jerky starts and stops, as she seemed to wrestle with the vehicle's highly responsive throttle.

Seraphel, a touch more cautious, was trying to get a handle on the myriad of buttons and switches her car boasted. Every time she pressed something, the car responded in unpredictable ways—sometimes hovering, other times dashing forward.

Morten, ironically the embodiment of Death, was the voice of caution. "Slow down! Get a feel for your vehicles first!" he shouted, as he tried to navigate a steady path.

But his warning came too late. Cassian, lost in the thrill and unfamiliar with the brakes, charged straight towards Morten at breakneck speed. Morten tried to swerve out of the way, but in his haste, he clipped the top of a tree, sending his car spiraling towards the ground.

The deafening crash that followed had everyone freezing in their tracks. Cassian's face was a shade paler, guilt evident in his eyes.

Liora winced at the sight of Morten's damaged vehicle, commenting dryly, "Perhaps we should've started with bicycles."

Morten, crawling out from his crumpled car, shot Cassian a look of irritation. "Cassian! We're supposed to bring destruction to Earth, not each other!"

Cassian, looking genuinely apologetic, replied, "Sorry, Morten. I got carried away. But hey, at least we know the airbags work!"

Seraphel, ever the pragmatist, sighed, "Morten, come with me. We can't waste any more time."

Morten nodded, joining Seraphel in her car. With a collective decision to move at a more controlled pace, the Horsemen took time to familiarize themselves with the basics of their vehicles.

As the horsemen successfully parked, Ezriel approached them, his expression softening, "You've all been chosen for this mission because of the unique strengths and qualities you possess. I have faith in each of you. Remember, it's not about the steeds or the cars; it's about the purpose. It's about passion. Be the best you that you can be. Don't let anyone get you down. Don't be small, be big. Be as big as you are. It takes big hearts and big courage to do this challenging apocalyptic stuff. Own it, be it, and live it. You can do this. I believe in you."

As the Horsemen zoomed off, a trail of celestial energy in their wake, Liora turned to Ezriel, confusion evident on her face. "What was that?"

"It's positive reinforcement or something," Ezriel responded with a shrug. "I've been learning about it from my podcasts."

Liora raised an eyebrow, "Do you think it will work?"

Ezriel sighed, his gaze following the fading trails of the Horsemen, "Only the end of time will tell."

# CHAPTER 16

# DOOMSDAY
# DIRECTIONS

The city's midday sun glinted off skyscrapers, illuminating the bustling sidewalks. People swarmed the streets, a sea of faces lost in their own worlds. But amid this urban maze, a familiar figure stood out - Larry, the Apocalyptic Street Preacher.

"The end is upon us!" Larry boomed, trying to cut through the rhythmic hum of the urban symphony. "The Horsemen have arrived!"

He had the rugged look of a man who'd spent countless days under the sun and wind, preaching his message. His messy hair, streaked with shades of silver, crowned a face deeply etched with lines of fervor and weariness. His piercing blue eyes seemed to carry a weight, a deep conviction, that was hard to ignore, even if you disagreed with his prophecies.

"The end is neigh! Carpe Diem!" Larry bellowed, voice carrying over the symphony of honking cars and distant conversations. He waved his weather-beaten Bible, as if it were a beacon of warning.

A little boy, holding his mother's hand, pointed at Larry. "Not this again," he whined, a hint of annoyance in his tone.

The mother, a woman in her thirties with a tired yet kind face, patted the boy's head. "Just ignore him, hun. We've heard it all before."

As the pair moved on, a sleek, dark vehicle pulled slowly alongside Larry. The window hummed down, revealing Seraphel's striking face, framed by cascading waves of hair. Beside her, Morten's hawkish eyes scanned the surroundings with a mix of curiosity and mild frustration.

"Hey," Seraphel called out, her voice dripping with sweetness, but a hint of impatience underneath, "Any idea where we can find parking around here?"

Larry, momentarily distracted from his sermon, turned to face the inquirer. His heart skipped a beat as he locked eyes with Seraphel, something primal within him screaming that these were not ordinary beings.

Without uttering a word, he dropped his Bible and bolted, feet pounding against the concrete.

Seraphel, reacting quickly, gunned the engine, and the car lurched forward. They weaved through the traffic, the powerful vehicle purring like a predatory cat as they pursued the fleeing preacher.

It was a strange sight — the Apocalyptic Street Preacher being chased down by a luxury car in broad daylight. Larry, driven by pure adrenaline, took a sharp turn into a narrow alley, hoping to shake them off. But the car, with its impressive agility, skidded right behind him.

Finally, at the alley's dead end, Larry found himself cornered. Seraphel and Morten, with synchronized grace, emerged from the car. They approached the panting preacher, expressions a blend of bemusement and concern.

"What the hell, man," Seraphel began, her voice now soothing, "we just wanted directions."

Morten nodded, "We're a bit lost. All these human constructs... it's confusing."

Larry stood in shock.

Seraphel added, "Who are you?"

Larry, tembeling in fear mustard the courage to speak, "I… I am Larry. But you can call me the Apocalyptic Street Preacher."

Searphel, "Yeah, we're not going to call you that, Larry."

Larry, heart still racing, looked between them, realization dawning. "You're... you're them."

"We are," Seraphel confirmed with a smile, "Now, how about you hop in and show us where to start?"

As Larry hesitated, Morten added, "It's just parking, for now."

Awestruck and overwhelmed, Larry found himself reluctantly agreeing, marking the beginning of an unexpected alliance.

Morten nodded, "We're a bit lost. All these human constructs... it's confusing."

Larry stood frozen, eyes darting between the two figures.

Seraphel leaned in, narrowing her eyes, "Who are you?"

Larry, trembling in fear, mustered the courage to speak, "I… I am Larry. But you can call me the Apocalyptic Street Preacher."

Seraphel smirked, "Yeah, we're not going to call you that, Larry."

Larry, heart still racing, looked between them, realization dawning. "You're... you're them."

"We are," Seraphel confirmed with a smile, "Now, how about you hop in and show us where to start?"

Larry took a step back, shaking his head vigorously. "No, no. I think I'll pass. Thank you."

Morten tilted his head, assessing Larry with an intensity that was unsettling. "You recognized us," he observed. "You're the only one who did. That means you can help."

Larry swallowed hard, "I just... I just preach about it. I don't actually know where you should begin!"

Seraphel's eyes gleamed with a hint of mischief. "Perhaps, but your knowledge of the prophecies might be useful. And we could use a guide."

"But I—"

Before Larry could protest further, Morten swiftly moved from the car, his hand firmly grasping Larry's upper arm. "We insist."

Larry's attempts to pull away were futile; Morten's grip was unyielding, otherworldly in strength. The street preacher was guided—practically shoved—into the back seat of the vehicle.

Morten leaned forward, locking eyes with the terrified man. "Relax, Larry. You might just become the most essential person on Earth. For the moment, at least."

Seraphel returned to the driver's seat, starting the car with a smooth purr. The vehicle rolled forward, with Larry sandwiched between two of the most powerful entities to ever walk the Earth, wondering how he'd become the unlikely guide for the onset of the apocalypse.

# CHAPTER 17

# APOCALYPTIC APPETITES

In a bustling mall food court, Elara sat alone, her eyes scanning the scene before her with increasing disgust. She saw families with trays piled high, toddlers throwing french fries, teenagers snapping selfies with their bubble teas, and adults shoveling fast food into their mouths as if in a race against time. To her, it was a spectacle of excess, a microcosm of the gluttony that plagued humanity.

The air was thick with the smell of grease, fried dough, and artificial sweeteners. People laughed and chatted, oblivious to the wastefulness of their indulgence. Elara could see half-eaten meals discarded, food dropped on the floor, and wrappers abandoned carelessly on tables. Her hands clenched involuntarily. She was the epitome of scarcity, and this blatant disregard for resources struck a chord deep within her.

Her gaze zeroed in on one table that epitomized everything she found repulsive. It was cluttered with dishes from various eateries: pizza boxes stacked atop each other, containers from Asian takeout joints, and wrappers from fast-food burgers. Sodas, milkshakes, and smoothies in varying stages of consumption surrounded the food. The sheer volume of it all was staggering, especially for a table that could only seat four.

With a deep breath to steady herself, Elara rose and walked toward the table, her footsteps deliberate. As she reached it, contemplating the enormity of the waste, a voice came from behind her.

"Ah, you found my table. Good. I was getting bored eating alone."

She turned around to find Cassian, grinning like a Cheshire cat. His eyes met hers as he sauntered over from the direction of the restrooms.

"You're kidding, right?" Elara's eyes were wide, her voice tinged with disbelief. "All of this is yours?"

Cassian chuckled. "Well, I wanted to sample a little bit of everything. Variety is the spice of life, as they say."

"Sample? This isn't a sample; this is a buffet," Elara retorted, her voice laced with disapproval.

"Oh, lighten up, Elara. We're here to understand humanity, remember? And from what I see, they love their indulgences."

Elara shook her head. "This isn't indulgence. This is wasteful. Do you have any idea how many go hungry while others dine like this?"

Cassian shrugged, seemingly unaffected by her disdain. "That's the duality of human existence, isn't it? Pleasure and pain, abundance and lack. That's what makes them interesting."

Elara looked at him, then back at the table piled high with food. "If this is what you find 'interesting,' then we are far from ready for what comes next."

Cassian leaned in closer, his eyes locking onto hers. "Oh, I'm always ready for what comes next. The question is, are they?" He gestured to the crowd around them, still engrossed in their own worlds of consumption and waste.

Elara sighed deeply, contemplating the immense task that lay ahead of them. And for a brief moment, amid the noise and chaos of the food court, both Horsemen stood in silence, acutely aware of the ticking clock that was humanity's time on Earth.

Elara folded her arms, leaning slightly against the table's edge. "So, what's your next move, Cassian?"

His smile faded a bit, replaced by a thoughtful expression. "I've got something big in mind. Ever heard of Vladimir Putin?"

Elara raised an eyebrow. "Of course. The Russian leader. Why?"

Cassian leaned in, his voice dropping to a conspiratorial whisper. "I'm going to break into his office."

Elara blinked in surprise. "You're kidding. That's one of the most secure places on Earth! How do you even plan to get in there?"

Cassian smirked, confidence radiating from him. "Let's just say I've got some connections that could prove useful. Besides, causing a bit of chaos at such high levels will send ripples across the globe. Imagine the anarchy that'll ensue."

Elara pursed her lips, clearly skeptical. "It's high risk. But if you pull it off, it might give us the advantage we need. As for me, I'm focusing on the world's rivers."

Cassian's eyes widened slightly. "You're planning to... dam them?"

She nodded, a glint of determination in her eyes. "Exactly. The Nile, the Amazon, the Yangtze. I'll place barriers, obstructing the flow. Entire cities and civilizations will suffer. They'll be crippled, yearning for what they took for granted."

Cassian pondered on this for a moment. "A bold move, but it might just work. You always were one for big gestures."

Elara smirked, a hint of a smile playing on her lips. "And you were always one for the theatrics. Breaking into Putin's office? Classic Cassian."

He laughed. "We each have our ways. Together, they won't stand a chance."

Elara gave him a dubious look, pointing a finger at him. "You're not going to…"

Cassian held up his hands defensively, chuckling. "No, no. I'm not going to stab his dick."

# CHAPTER 18

# Of Tiny Apartments and Human Quirks

The ceiling fan whirred slowly above as the trio sat in Larry's small apartment. With its faded wallpaper and worn-out furniture, the apartment felt even smaller with two supernatural beings crammed inside. The blinds were drawn, but occasional slivers of city lights streamed in, revealing the dust dancing in the air.

Larry was perched on an old armchair, clutching a mug of tea. Seraphel, with her ethereal presence, had gracefully chosen the window seat, while Morten, ever so awkward, was sprawled on the floor, his long legs stretched out.

A distant rumble alerted them, and as the train approached, the noise grew deafening. They waited, sipping their beverages in silence, each lost in thought. Finally, as the train passed, Larry spoke up, "That happens quite frequently. Old city infrastructure, you know?"

Morten frowned, trying to adjust to the different nuances of human life. "This... train, it's a mode of transportation?"

Seraphel smirked. "Yes, no," she began, confusing Morten even further, "it's more than that. It's like... a symbol of human persistence and routine."

Morten blinked. "So... is that a yes or a no?"

Larry chuckled, "No, yeah, it's both. It's a transportation thing, but also, as Seraphel said, a symbol of sorts."

Morten looked utterly baffled. "Why wouldn't you just say yes or no? Why add the extra?"

Larry leaned forward, animated. "That's just how humans talk. It's a nuance. Like when someone asks if you're coming to the party and you say, 'yeah, no' – it means you're not coming. But 'no, yeah' means you are."

Morten squinted, processing. "So... 'yeah, no' is no, and 'no, yeah' is yes?"

Seraphel laughed, "Exactly! Humans aren't always straightforward."

"But it seems so... unnecessary," Morten pondered.

Larry sighed, "Well, humans are complex. Our language, our behaviors, our traditions, they're all layered. We don't always say what we mean directly. That's the beauty and confusion of it."

Morten attempted to understand. "So, if I said, 'yes, no,' I'm disagreeing?"

Seraphel and Larry exchanged amused glances.

"No, yeah," Larry confirmed.

Morten groaned, "This is going to be harder than I thought."

As another train roared by, forcing another pause in their conversation, the room filled with the lingering reverberations before they eventually faded away. Larry seized the opportunity to steer the conversation in a new direction.

"So, if you don't mind me asking, what's the big plan here? The grand design for the end of the world?" Larry's voice wavered between genuine curiosity and a tinge of anxiety.

Seraphel leaned back, crossing her legs, her eyes twinkling. "I'll draw lines, divide lands, and create borders. Pitting humans against each other, making them fight for territories, letting greed consume them."

Larry's eyes widened, and he opened his mouth to say something, but another train roared by. The words died on his lips, and he waited for the train to pass.

Morten, who had been deep in thought, finally spoke up. "As for me, I'm not entirely sure yet. I've been contemplating several avenues. You see, the human psyche is so complex, so rich in its paradoxes. There's many layers. I'm learning that death doesn't only exist when a life vanishes, but also in moments. It's a very introspective journey. I'm considering tapping into—"

Seraphel interjected, her voice dripping with impatience, "Larry, how often did you say these trains come by?"

Larry let out a quiet chuckle, "Not often enough, apparently."

Morten paused, looking mildly affronted. "I was merely expressing the intricate considerations—"

"Indeed, you were," Seraphel cut him off, shooting Larry an eye roll that spoke volumes.

Larry chuckled again, feeling a little more relaxed than he should, given the gravity of the subject matter. It was becoming increasingly evident that even celestial beings tasked with apocalypse had their quirks and, dare he say, vulnerabilities. For a moment, Larry pondered the irony—entities bent on humanity's doom were struggling to understand its intricacies.

"Alright," Larry finally said, "Why don't we regroup, maybe take a moment to collect our thoughts. I can make more tea, if you'd like?"

Seraphel leaned in, her face solemn, eyes piercing. "Larry, given the circumstances, and our mission, we've come to a decision." She paused for effect, letting the weight of her words hang in the air. "We believe consuming human flesh might give us a better understanding of your kind."

Larry froze, his mouth agape. "You...you want to eat me?"

Morten chimed in, nodding seriously, "Yes. It's a method we've considered. You know, to truly understand one's adversary, one must walk in their shoes. Or in this case, ingest them."

Larry's eyes darted from Seraphel to Morten and then to the apartment's only exit. His thoughts raced, frantically searching for a way out. "I... I can cook? How about a steak or something? I have some tofu in the fridge. That's almost like human, right?"

Seraphel pretended to ponder this for a moment, her expression contemplative. "Tofu, you say? Interesting proposition."

Morten pretended to shudder, "Too chewy for my taste."

They held the tension for just a moment longer before Seraphel burst into laughter. "Oh, Larry, your face!" she exclaimed between giggles.

Morten joined in, his laughter deep and infectious. "We jest, Larry! We jest. Although, I must say, your offer of tofu was truly entertaining."

Larry, still catching his breath, managed a weak chuckle. "That was... twisted. You two have a very dark sense of humor."

Seraphel winked. "Apocalyptic humor, remember?"

Larry sighed with relief. "Tea it is then. Maybe some biscuits?"

As they settled down, Larry watched as Morten started inspecting the bed, pressing down on the mattress with a critical expression. "Is it firm?" he asked. "I've been having some celestial back issues lately."

Larry raised an eyebrow. "Celestial back issues?"

Morten shrugged. "It's a thing. Do you mind if we share the bed? I promise I won't take much space. We can go head-to-feet if that's more comfortable."

Larry raised an eyebrow, searching Morten's face for any hint of deception. "Head-to-feet?"

Morten nodded, a hint of eagerness in his eyes, "Yes, it'll be perfectly civil. I promise."

Larry took a deep breath, his mind racing. The idea of sleeping beside the embodiment of death wasn't his ideal situation, especially after the evening's events. Still, Morten's insistence seemed genuine, and Larry had to admit there was a certain allure to learning more about these beings.

"Okay," Larry began cautiously, "but if your feet end up anywhere near my face... that's a boundary, alright?"

Morten grinned, exposing his otherworldly sharp teeth. "Deal. And don't worry about the feet. It's a human thing; celestial beings don't have foot odor. Much."

Seraphel laughed as she moved toward the window. "Sleep tight, you two. And remember, Morten, no midnight snacks without me.

With that, she climbed outside to sleep on fire escape, leaving the two men inside. Larry glanced over at Morten, now settling into the twin sized bed, the surrealism of the moment hitting him once more.

As he climbed into the opposite end of the bed, he tried to find some semblance of comfort in the situation. On one hand, his apocalyptic prophecies had validation. On the other, he was sharing his bed with death incarnate. As Morten's soft snores filled the room, Larry found solace in one small fact: at least the horseman's feet, celestial or not, weren't that smelly. Well, mostly.

# CHAPTER 19

# ELARA'S
# REVELATION

Outside the mall, the two horsemen shared a brief, intense moment of acknowledgement. A nod from Cassian and a piercing gaze from Elara served as their unspoken farewell. They had jobs to do, parts of the plan to enact. As Cassian turned to head eastward, Elara set her sights on the West Coast of the U.S.

She maneuvered her flying car gracefully, letting the technology take over as she crossed state lines and national borders. A shimmering expanse of desert lay beneath her, its vastness and arid beauty capturing her attention. The simulator had taught her that the vibrant and fertile lands of Mexico would be the perfect place to commence her famine-driven assault on humanity.

Elara decided to make her landing near a small village. As the flying car settled onto the dry ground, a cloud of dust rose around her, the fine particles sparkling in the dying light.

Elara was met with curious and cautious eyes from the villagers. Their initial wariness, however, was overshadowed by an unmistakable weariness. There were no overflowing markets or bountiful farms as she had anticipated. Instead, the land was parched, and the faces around her told a tale of a persistent struggle against the unyielding landscape.

Approaching a woman who was drawing water from a nearly depleted well, Elara inquired, "Where are the plentiful farms and the rich lands I've heard about?"

The woman, shielding her eyes from the setting sun, replied, "Those days are long gone, señorita. Our rivers are drying up, and the rains are few and far between. The land no longer yields as it used to. We've had to adapt, find new ways to survive."

Elara, taken aback, pressed further. "But Mexico... I was told it was a land of abundance."

"Once, perhaps. But climate change, over-extraction, and other factors have taken their toll. We do what we can, but the old ways, the times of plenty, they are memories now."

Elara nodded, processing the information, her celestial essence absorbing the gravity of the situation. A breeze rustled through the sparse vegetation, and she could feel the aridness in the air, a tangible representation of the land's thirst.

"Thank you for sharing this with me," she whispered, her voice soft and distant, as if speaking to herself more than anyone else. The woman simply nodded, her gaze following Elara as she turned towards her flying car. A moment of connection passed between the two, an understanding beyond words.

As Elara climbed back into the vehicle, her thoughts were turbulent. The simulation had prepared her for a world of excess, but the reality was far more complex. She realized her strategy needed to evolve; the world she had anticipated was not the world she was in.

With a silent determination, she directed her flying car to ascend and follow the flow of the river, tracing its path as it weaved and twisted through the landscape. She was on a new mission, to understand more about this world, to see where the water led and why.

The river's winding journey took her north, past changing terrains and landscapes. The sun, in its eternal dance, began its descent, casting a golden hue over the land. The waters below reflected a tapestry of oranges and purples, leading Elara to the vast expanses of California.

With the scorching sun blazing in the sky, Elara found herself amidst the vast expanse of vineyards that stretched as far as the eye could see. The air carried the sweet scent of ripening grapes, a stark contrast to the arid landscape she had witnessed just a while ago in Mexico. Ahead of her, a sign greeted her: "Welcome to California's Wine Country."

Her eyes shifted from the sign to the lush vineyards, and then to the active sprinklers spraying water across the plants. As droplets caught the sunlight, they refracted it into ephemeral rainbows, creating a mesmerizing display. But the sheer scale of the artificial hydration left her puzzled.

"Why would they plant so much in a desert?" she muttered to herself, trying to grasp the logic behind the scene, "Have they not heard of location-appropriate crops?"

Just then, the sound of footsteps approached. Turning her gaze, she met the eyes of a middle-aged man with sun-kissed skin, wearing a straw hat and a friendly smile. "Well, hello there!" he greeted, extending a hand in her direction, "First time in California?"

Elara, still trying to piece things together, replied cautiously, "Yes, and I'm rather confused. Aren't you concerned about using so much water here?"

The man, now identified by the name tag on his overalls as Joe, let out a hearty laugh. "Oh, we have our ways! Advanced irrigation, recycled water, you name it."

She tilted her head, curious, "But why? There are places with abundant water where these crops would thrive naturally. Why force a square peg into a round hole?"

Joe scratched his head, chuckling, "Well, the wine tastes great, the tourists love it, and hey, it's tradition."

Elara raised an eyebrow, "Tradition to... grow plants in a desert?"

He shrugged, a smile playing on his lips, "Well, when you put it that way, it does sound a bit silly."

Following her gaze to one of the active sprinklers, Elara commented, "And those! Tiny man-made rainstorms? Is that your solution to making a desert bloom?"

Joe laughed again, a rich, genuine sound, "Well, it's more complex than that, but yeah, something like that."

Elara shook her head, an amused smile forming, "Humans truly are a peculiar species. You change the environment to suit your needs instead of adapting to it."

Joe winked, pointing towards the vast vineyard behind him, "Well, when you've got a taste for good wine, you go to great lengths!"

Elara's car glided gracefully over the Californian desert, but as she flew northward, a peculiarly verdant patch amidst the beige expanse caught her eye. From above, it looked like meticulously designed patches of green, dotted with sand and tiny ponds. Intrigued, she descended for a closer look.

As her feet touched the soft grass, she noticed a man in the distance, swinging a club and hitting a small white ball. Beside him, a cart loaded with clubs and a fluttering flag.

The man, noticing Elara's car and her evident confusion, approached with a broad smile. "Hey there! A bit lost, are we?"

Elara looked around, still trying to make sense of the place. "I'm Elara. This is... extraordinary. What is this place?"

The man chuckled, "Name's Max. Welcome to our golf course!"

"Golf?" she echoed, her brows furrowing.

"Yeah, golf!" Max beamed, raising his club. "A game where you try to get this little ball," he pointed at the white dimpled sphere at his feet, "into a series of holes in as few strokes as possible."

Elara glanced around, taking in the vast stretch of vibrant land. "All this... for a game?"

Max laughed, "You sound just like my eco-conscious friends. But yes, it's a game loved by many. Though," he sighed, looking around with a hint of guilt, "maintaining these courses does require a lot of water. Probably more than we should be using, especially in California."

She remembered the parched fields she'd seen in Mexico and the desert vineyards. "I've witnessed the dire need for water just south of here. This seems... excessive."

Max looked sheepish, "It's a luxury, no doubt. Many argue we could use land and resources in better ways. But it's a tradition, a passion for many. And, well, in California, water has always been gold."

Elara raised an eyebrow, "Gold?"

Max chuckled, "Gold. Precious metal. A couple of centuries back, folks came rushing here believing they'd strike it rich. But now, the gold isn't the yellow metal anymore. It's this," he knelt, scooping up a handful of moist soil, letting the water seep through his fingers, "Water."

Elara's thoughts immediately went back to Mexico and the parched fields she had witnessed. "I've seen the consequences downstream. Lands drying up, crops failing."

Max sighed, looking guilty, "We follow a saying here: 'Whiskey's for drinking, water's for fighting.'"

Elara's brows furrowed as she took to the air again, her car gliding effortlessly above the ground. She followed the course of the river, and with each twist and turn, another dam loomed into view. The sight was far from what she had expected. Large concrete structures, some with vast reservoirs and others mere barriers, dotted the river's pathway. It felt as though humans had already imposed their own apocalypse on the land.

"I came to make an impact, to bring about chaos," she muttered to herself, the realization sinking in. "But they've done it themselves."

She accelerated, the wind whipping past as her car soared higher. As the dams whizzed by, she tried to keep count but soon gave up, the sheer number making the task impossible. The once wild and mighty river seemed tamed, every drop accounted for and allocated.

The landscape beneath her began to blur with speed, a mosaic of artificial lakes, barren stretches, and green patches. Elara's mind raced. If humans had already done such a thorough job of controlling the water, what more could she do? What was the point of her mission if the chaos she intended to sow was already deeply rooted in human action?

Suddenly, an intense emotion welled up in her—a mix of frustration, confusion, and a touch of admiration for humanity's relentless drive. For a species so intent on survival, they sure had a way of walking the line between creation and destruction.

As miles turned into mere moments, Elara's car reached breakneck speeds. The last dam she glimpsed had a familiar shape—a curved barrier holding back a vast blue expanse. Recognizing it as the Hoover Dam, she realized she'd nearly traversed the length of the river. The vast Lake Mead lay behind the dam, shimmering in the midday sun, a testament to human engineering.

With a forceful exhale, Elara eased up on the accelerator, allowing her vehicle to coast and gradually slow down. Her confusion deepened. The clarity she sought eluded her. She was supposed to be a harbinger of the end times, but now she wondered: were humans already their own apocalypse?

She parked her flying car atop a mesa, overlooking the vast expanse of the Colorado River basin. The setting sun painted the sky in hues of orange and pink. For a moment, Elara felt small, insignificant in the grand timeline of Earth's story.

# CHAPTER 20

# INFILTRATING THE KREMLIN

The evening haze was settling over Moscow, leaving a thin veil of mystery over its cold, historic streets. The amber glow from the overhead street lamps formed a dome of light under the underpass, which otherwise was enveloped in an inky darkness.

Cassian stood patiently, the collar of his trench coat turned up to shield his face from the cold and any prying eyes. The muted echo of footsteps reached his ears. They were deliberate, heavy—like the march of a soldier but with a touch of stealth.

A silhouette began to emerge from the dense mist—a man, tall and broad, also cloaked in a trench coat. The very sight of him commanded both fear and respect. Cassian felt his pulse quicken, but he forced himself to remain composed, recalling Ezriel's words: "Trust the connection. He will get you inside."

The approaching man's eyes remained hidden beneath the brim of his hat, but Cassian could sense them studying him intently. As they were about to meet, the stranger dramatically pulled his coat open. Cassian stiffened, half-expecting to see an array of weapons. Instead, a janitorial uniform, complete with nametag, was revealed.

"Password?" The voice carried the weight of a heavy Russian accent, bringing to mind every Cold War spy movie Cassian had ever watched.

Stifling his nerves, Cassian responded, "Scrotal Sword."

The thick silence that followed was soon broken by the janitor's emerging grin. The Russian accent vanished, replaced by the tones of the British Isles. "All right, mate. You can call me Ted."

Cassian frowned, his eyebrows knitting together in disbelief. "Ted? Of all the names... I was expecting a Boris or Ivan... or maybe a Dmitry. But, Ted?"

Ted chuckled heartily, "Got something against the name Ted?"

"It's just..." Cassian began, searching for the right words, "It's not very climactic."

"Well, mate, I assure you, when it comes to climax, I never disappoint," Ted winked.

Cassian looked flustered. "That's not—"

Ted held up a hand, "Save it. You're here to get into the Kremlin, right?"

Eyeing the janitorial equipment, Cassian retorted, "You're actually a janitor?"

Ted, unperturbed, nodded. "That I am. Is there a problem?"

"No, no, of course not," Cassian backtracked. "It's a noble profession. It's just... unexpected. And again, not very climactic."

Ted smirked, "Life's full of surprises, mate. And just to clear things up, I have no issues in the climax department."

Cassian took a deep breath, "Thanks, Ted. But given the circumstances, I think I'll take my chances alone."


The early morning hours found the sky over Moscow cloaked in a smoky gray, hinting at a downpour. Cassian, concealed within the darkness of a nearby alleyway, eyed the towering red brick walls of the Kremlin with determination. He began his ascent, using a combination of gadgets and raw athletic prowess to scale the structure.

Once he reached a suitable entry point, a ventilation duct, he began his delicate process of removing the grate. The silence of the predawn city was only punctured by his own quiet breaths and the occasional hoot of an owl. Cassian slipped inside the vent, pulling the grate back into place behind him. The narrow metal corridor was cold, and the darkness inside was all-consuming. Cassian relied on his sense of touch, carefully crawling forward.

Hours seemed to pass, and Cassian felt the space around him getting even tighter. The maps hadn't indicated a constriction in this particular vent, and he realized with a sinking feeling that he might have taken a wrong turn. Every attempt to move forward seemed to wedge him further in place. Panic started to gnaw at the edge of his mind; the claustrophobic atmosphere felt like it was squeezing the very air from his lungs.

His mind raced. Thoughts of being discovered, or worse, of dying a slow and undignified death in a ventilation shaft in the Kremlin flooded his thoughts. Cassian's breathing grew ragged as the weight of his predicament bore down on him. He had trained for numerous scenarios, but this was one situation he hadn't anticipated.

Just as despair was about to fully set in, Cassian heard an unexpected noise—a soft sloshing sound. He felt small droplets hit his face. Instinctively, he tasted one—it was stale and slightly dirty. The sound of rubber on metal echoed in the confines of the shaft.

Suddenly, Cassian was jarred by a forceful prod to his head. A mop handle. Then, with an exclamation and the sound of sliding fabric, Ted came barreling down from above, colliding with Cassian's trapped form. The impact, though painful, was enough to free Cassian from his awkward position.

The weight and momentum of the two men was too much for the shaft to handle. With a series of groans and creaks, the vent began to give way. The world spun as they plummeted, crashing through layers of ductwork. With one final, deafening crash, they burst through a ceiling, debris and dust billowing around them.

When the dust settled, Cassian and Ted found themselves lying amidst the remnants of their crash landing, in the heart of the Kremlin. Both took a moment to regain their composure and grasp the reality of their unexpected entry.

Ted grinned cheekily, helping Cassian to his feet. "Well, my friend, told you I'm good at what I do."

"Ted... wow, you really—"

"Know how to climax?" Ted interrupted with a smirk.

"Ugh, yeah."

"What do you think my mop is for?" Ted winked, making Cassian groan in response.

Their banter was cut short by the distant sound of footsteps and hushed voices, growing louder with every second. The urgency of their mission came rushing back, and they exchanged a knowing glance.

"Time to move," whispered Cassian.

Ted saluted with a smirk. "Good luck, and if you need me for anything, call me."

Cassian paused briefly, nodding. "Okay, thank you."

Ted leaned in slightly, his voice a soft, playful murmur. "And," he added, "I mean anything at all."

"Yeah, got it," Cassian replied, rolling his eyes and suppressing a smirk. "Now, get the fuck out of here, Ted."

---

Cassian turned, dashing off towards Putin's office while Ted made his agile escape into another vent, disappearing as quickly and mysteriously as he had come.

# The Breakfast Revelation

The early morning rays illuminated the urban landscape as Seraphel stirred on the fire escape. The city hummed with its typical cacophony of distant cars, birds chirping, and the distant drone of city life. The cool breeze made her shiver momentarily before she remembered her celestial origins. A warm, rich scent wafted up, capturing her attention.

She pushed herself up and climbed back inside Larry's apartment, the aroma growing stronger. The scene that greeted her was... domestic. Larry and Morten sat at a cramped table in the middle of a sunlit room, their faces animated. A glorious spread of food was laid out before them: plump bagels laden with cream cheese and glistening lox, stacks of golden pancakes dripping with maple syrup, crispy bacon strips, and an array of fruits.

Seraphel blinked, "Did I miss the memo about breakfast?"

Morten, with a mouth full of pancake, gestured enthusiastically at the food. "It's delightful, Seraphel. I never got to experience the charm of such morning delicacies during my eons."

Larry chuckled, pouring a cup of steaming coffee. "There's something remarkably human about enjoying a hearty breakfast. Please, join us."

Taking a seat and reaching for a bagel, Seraphel began to outline her plan. "I've been pondering my role as Conquest. My strategy is to further divide mankind. Borders that separate lands and ideologies, resources that only a few control, pushing others into desperation. Mankind will forever be locked in a cycle of wanting, needing, taking."

Larry looked pensive, stirring his coffee. "A world where everyone desires more and would trample over others to get it? Where conflict is endless, and harmony is but a distant dream?"

Seraphel nodded, "Exactly. Through envy and greed, mankind will conquer one another perpetually."

There was a heavy pause before Larry finally spoke up. "Seraphel, that's... that's already happened."

She looked taken aback, "What do you mean?"

Larry leaned forward, his expression earnest. "Borders have been drawn, resources monopolized, wars waged over power and control. Humanity has been in a cycle of conquest for centuries."

Seraphel's brows furrowed in disbelief. "I thought I was introducing something new, a twist in their tale."

Morten, setting down his fork, added, "Perhaps our perspectives are different because we've seen millennia unfold. To us, a few centuries might seem brief. But to humans, it's their entire history."

Larry spread the map across the table, the continents and their boundaries displayed vividly. "Borders," he began, "are humanity's way of laying claim to land, resources, and even ideologies."

He pointed to a continent. "Here, at the scale of countries, we see vast swathes of land divided and claimed by nations, each protecting their sovereignty, each jealously guarding what they believe is rightfully theirs. Wars have been waged, lives lost, all for the sake of these invisible lines."

Moving his fingers to zoom into regions, Larry continued, "And it doesn't stop there. Within these countries are states, provinces, divided further still, each with its own government, its own laws, its own identity."

He then zoomed in closer, showing towns and cities. "Here we have towns and municipalities. Each governing its populace, each ensuring that its interests are maintained. And within these towns, further divisions."

Seraphel sat silent, absorbing the reality Larry was painting.

Morten chimed in, "And resources, I assume, are the lifeblood of these divisions?"

Larry nodded, "Exactly. Now, let's talk about resources." He pulled out another document – it looked like a pie chart. "Water, minerals, oil, arable land... these are just some of the resources nations fight for. Control over them can determine the power dynamics of the world."

Pointing to a section of the chart, he continued, "Freshwater, for instance. Many parts of the world are experiencing shortages. Countries with abundant freshwater sources wield significant power."

He moved to another section. "Then there's oil, the black gold. Wars have been fought, regimes toppled, all for control over this precious resource."

Morten looked grim. "It's as if mankind is set on a path of endless competition, always wanting more, never satisfied."

Seraphel sighed, "I thought my role would be to introduce a new form of chaos. But it seems humanity has beaten me to it."

Larry nodded, "The desire to conquer, to control, it's an age-old trait of mankind. Your plans, as disruptive as they are, would only be intensifying what's already in place."

Seraphel's eyes hardened with determination. "I'm not here to just accelerate the inevitable. There must be a unique purpose to my role." She stood up abruptly, her chair scraping back loudly in the quiet room. "I need to think, to re-strategize. I won't accept redundancy."

She headed towards the door, pausing only to glance back at Morten, who was still looking contemplatively at the charts Larry had spread out. "Are you coming?"

Morten's attention shifted between Seraphel and Larry, his gaze pensive. "What will you do now, Larry?"

Larry shrugged, a wry smile on his lips. "Well, it's just another day for me. I'll probably head to my usual spot with my soapbox. Tell people the apocalypse is here. It's familiar, you know. Business as usual."

Morten's eyebrows rose, intrigued. "That actually sounds like fun. A bit of dramatic flair, proclaiming doom to the masses."

Seraphel's voice bore a hint of frustration. "Seriously, you're staying?"

Morten met her gaze evenly. "Death is everywhere, Seraphel."

She frowned, her brow knitting in confusion. "What does that even mean?"

He paused, considering his own words. "I don't know... yet."

Larry shifted uncomfortably, sensing the tension between the two. Seraphel sighed and shook her head. "Alright, Morten. Do as you see fit. But remember our mission."

With a final nod, she left, leaving Morten and Larry in a room thick with an unsaid understanding. Morten finally broke the silence. "Let's see what the world has to offer today, Larry."

Larry stood up from his chair with pride, clearly excited for Morten's company. "Come on, then. We've got a city to warn. The end is nigh!"

# CHAPTER 22

# The Unanticipated Savoir

The opulence of Putin's office was unmistakable: deep mahogany, golden embellishments, and paintings of Russia's past leaders framed by velvet drapes. A grand desk stood as the centerpiece, and the room emitted an aura of power. Cassian, taking it all in, noticed a beautifully crafted decorative sword mounted above the entrance door, its hilt encrusted with jewels.

As the distant echoes of footsteps grew nearer, Cassian quickly hid inside a sizable closet, leaving a small gap for him to view the room. He activated his recorder, ensuring to capture every word of the upcoming conversation. The door opened, revealing Vladimir Putin accompanied by a group of stern-looking officials.

"...Already in Ukraine, and the situation in Belarus isn't helping," an advisor warned.

"We have our plans in place. They need to know we're not playing games!" Putin's voice, cold and determined, filled the room.

"But Sir, the international consequences... if we push too hard..." another official started.

Putin slammed his fist on the table. "They've been undermining us for too long! It's time they understand Russia's might!"

As the conversation continued, the tension in the room grew immensely. Talks of alliances, troops, and covert operations filled the room, building a tapestry of impending doom.

"It's not just a matter of might! It's about mutual destruction! If you send the nukes, they will retaliate," an advisor argued.

With a determined tone, Putin retorted, "Let them! Let the world see the consequences of challenging Mother Russia!"

As Cassian watched from the closet, he realized the magnitude of the decision that hung in the balance. The room's energy shifted, and it became evident that Putin was moments away from pressing a dreaded button that would irrevocably change the world.

Acting on impulse, Cassian flung the closet door open, drawing the eyes of everyone in the room. With a fluid motion, he seized the decorative sword from above the door and advanced with deadly precision. One by one, the officials fell, taken by surprise and unable to defend against the swift and relentless Horseman.

In the midst of the chaos, Putin managed to evade Cassian's onslaught, fleeing from the office with fear evident in his eyes. The echo of his hurried footsteps faded into the distance.

Cassian, breathing heavily, surveyed the carnage. He felt an odd sense of pride—ironically, the Horseman who trained to sow chaos had just prevented it. The world would not end this day, not in a blinding flash of nuclear fire. Their mission had a larger purpose, one that transcended the whims of any one man.

With the recorder still in hand, capturing the eerie silence of the room, Cassian felt a strange sensation in the pit of his stomach. Here he was, trained and primed to ignite the flames of war, only to discover that those flames already raged without his influence.

His mind raced back to another lesson from the Apocalypse Academy, one that resonated deeply now. It was not just about the physical wars waged with weapons and soldiers; true chaos and destruction lay in the wars of the mind, the battles of the heart, the conflicts that tore souls apart.

The memory in the simulator struck Cassian, "War isn't just about borders and bombs. It's also within." Taking a deep breath, he whispered to himself, "I need to go to America." The world's superpower, with its world wide cultural influence, it would be the perfect battleground for this new strategy.

# CHAPTER 23

# THE SECRETS BENEATH

Elara headed northeast, letting the diverse landscapes of North America play out beneath her. The vast plains gave way to bustling cities, and soon the sprawling forests of the East Coast loomed below. Vibrant shades of green carpeted the earth as thick canopies shielded the ground from the midday sun. Between the trees, she could spot houses, each nestled into its own little clearing, surrounded by nature. This region seemed like a stark contrast to the parched landscapes of the West.

She descended, attracted to a particularly verdant section of the forest. The ground was damp, streams crisscrossed the landscape, and the gentle hum of life was palpable. In the distance, she spotted a well, a testament to the abundant underground water source.

Just as she was about to enact her initial strategy, an argument between two humans caught her attention. She approached cautiously, taking cover behind a thick oak, her celestial essence absorbing their heated words.

"I'm telling you, Frank, you need to get your well water checked!" the younger man exclaimed, frustration evident in his voice.

"And I told you, I've been drinking this water for thirty years. Do I look like I have seven heads to you?" Frank retorted, a mocking tone in his voice.

"Cancer doesn't give you seven heads, Frank!" The younger man was clearly exasperated.

The two continued their banter, with Frank adamantly resisting the idea of testing his water. As their voices rose, Elara couldn't help but intervene.

"Excuse me," she said, emerging from behind the tree. Both men turned to look at her, surprised. "I couldn't help but overhear. What is this 'PFAS' you speak of?"

The younger man, his face a mix of suspicion and curiosity, replied, "PFAS are a group of man-made chemicals. They've been used in various products over the years, from non-stick cookware to water-repellent clothing and even firefighting foams."

Frank huffed, "All these years, no issue, and now suddenly it's a big deal?"

Elara, intrigued, asked, "How did it end up in your groundwater?"

The younger man sighed, "It leaches. Over time, these chemicals have made their way into the soil and, eventually, our groundwater. They're persistent, meaning they don't break down easily. Long-term exposure can have health implications."

Frank waved his hand dismissively, "It's all a conspiracy. I feel fine."

Elara's gaze shifted between the two men. Here she was, ready to strike at the heart of humanity's water supply, only to discover that they were already poisoning themselves. The irony wasn't lost on her.

The younger man, noticing Elara's contemplative expression, asked, "You new around here? Haven't seen you before."

Elara nodded, choosing her words carefully, "I'm just passing through, trying to understand more about your world."

"Well," the younger man smirked, "Welcome to the East Coast, where even our purest resources have secrets."

Frank grumbled something inaudible and began walking away, leaving Elara with the younger man.

She took a moment, letting the weight of this new revelation sink in. It seemed that every corner of this world had its own set of challenges, often self-inflicted by the very beings she had come to challenge.

The younger man extended a hand, "I'm Ben, by the way."

Elara took his hand gently, her grace only slightly betraying her otherworldly nature. "Elara," she replied.

Ben nodded, acknowledging her presence. "What brings you to this neck of the woods?"

She looked slightly flustered, thinking quickly on her feet. "I'm doing a... umm... research report on famine. You know, like how to cause it."

Ben raised an eyebrow, clearly taken aback. "That's an... unusual topic. Most people want to prevent famine, not cause it."

Realizing her gaffe, Elara quickly tried to amend, "I meant, I'm studying the causes to understand the solutions better. But in understanding solutions, one must first deeply know the problems, right?"

Ben looked thoughtful for a moment. "That's a fair point. Well, if you're genuinely interested in famine, some of the most severe instances are in Africa."

Elara tilted her head, genuinely curious. "Why Africa?"

Ben sighed. "There's a myriad of reasons. Climate, for one. Many regions suffer from unpredictable rain patterns and droughts, especially in areas like the Sahel. Locust infestations are another major challenge. They can devour vast stretches of crops, leaving entire communities without food."

He paused, taking a breath. "And then there's water. Contaminated water is a severe issue in many parts. And while we are arguing about PFAS here, many places in Africa are struggling with waterborne diseases like cholera."

Elara looked down, a weight in her heart. "I had no idea," she admitted softly. "It seems I still have so much to learn about this world."

Ben smiled gently, "We all do. It's a vast, intricate planet. And while there's beauty and joy, there's also pain and challenges."

They walked together in silence for a moment. Elara glanced towards the horizon, deep in thought. All around her, the forest hummed with life, yet the weight of human actions weighed heavily upon the land.

Ben, sensing her contemplation, asked, "What will you do with your findings, Elara?"

Elara looked at him, her eyes shimmering with a cosmic depth. "I came here with a purpose. But every moment I spend on Earth, I realize the complexity of existence here. It's not just about taking or giving, but understanding."

Ben nodded, understanding in his eyes. "It's easy to see problems and try to find quick fixes. But the real solutions come from understanding, compassion, and collaboration."

A gentle breeze rustled the trees around them, birds sang in the distance, and for a moment, the world felt harmonious.

Ben looked at Elara for a moment before breaking the silence. "You know, in case you have more questions or just want to chat, can I have your phone number?"

Elara's eyes widened slightly, and she appeared momentarily off-balance. "Oh, um," she stammered, her cheeks flushing a shade of pink that looked quite foreign on her otherworldly face. "I don't actually have a phone. Or a number."

Ben raised an eyebrow, his lips curling into a playful smile. "No phone? You really are from a different world, aren't you?"

She chuckled softly, her flush deepening. "It seems I've overlooked some essentials during my time here. But I'll get one. I promise."

Ben, still smiling, jotted down his number on a scrap of paper and handed it to her. "Well, when you do, here's my number. Give me a call, okay?"

Elara carefully took the paper, looking at the digits as if they held some cosmic secret. "Thank you, Ben. I will."

With a nod, he said, "Good luck with your research report. And remember, there's more to Earth than meets the eye."

She smiled warmly. "I'm beginning to see that, thanks to people like you."

# CHAPTER 24

# THE MIRAGE OF PROSPERITY

In the heart of Manhattan, Seraphel's attention was caught by the sheen of sunlight reflecting off the polished exterior of a luxury car. A man, with slicked-back hair and a tailored suit, confidently stepped out, waving to the valet. His demeanor and the glint in his eye told a story of financial conquest.

Curious, Seraphel approached him, her otherworldly aura instantly making her captivating to the man. "Hello," she greeted. "You seem to have done well for yourself."

The man, taking a moment to assess the mysterious woman in front of him, smiled. "I get by. Name's Craig. And you are?"

"Seraphel. Would you be open to sharing a meal? I'd love to know more about your success."

Intrigued, Craig agreed. The two of them walked to a nearby upscale restaurant. Settling into plush seats, they ordered, and without wasting time, Seraphel probed, "Tell me about your conquests, Craig."

Craig chuckled, taking a sip of his wine. "This car you admire? Doesn't belong to me. It's a company car. But I have another one at home, though that's on a loan."

Seraphel leaned in, her curiosity piqued. "A loan?"

Craig nodded. "To build credit. You see, in this world, appearance is everything. I have a beautiful house overlooking the Hudson. But that too is on a mortgage."

"Why not own them outright?"

Craig shrugged. "Leverage. Also, the allure of wealth is more seductive than wealth itself. My ventures? Real estate trading. But the market isn't what it was. I have properties that are stuck, and the payments don't stop. My kids? They're in college, on student loans."

Seraphel paused, absorbing the revelations. "So, your conquest..."

"Is the art of looking rich. When you look successful, doors open. Opportunities come knocking. People are more willing to invest in a winner, even if that win is just a facade."

Seraphel studied Craig, realizing the weight he carried, the facade he maintained. His life was a balancing act on a tightrope of debts, appearances, and societal pressures.

As they wrapped up their meal, Seraphel thanked Craig for his time. "Your world has many layers," she mused. "And conquest isn't always about owning; sometimes, it's about portraying."

Craig looked at Seraphel, sensing a depth in her that he couldn't quite grasp. "You're not from around here, are you?"

She smiled enigmatically. "No, I'm not. And every day, I learn something new."

As they parted ways, Seraphel pondered the human desire to appear wealthy, the illusions they crafted, and the fragility of it all. Here, she realized, the conquest was intangible, and the battlefield was perception.

Manhattan's streets were bustling with energy, the cacophony of horns, lively chatter, and distant sirens creating a unique symphony. Yet, amidst this liveliness, by the iconic bronze Charging Bull, Seraphel noticed a stark contrast: a young man, sitting dejectedly with tear-streaked cheeks.

Drawn to his evident distress, she approached him gently. "Why so troubled amidst such grandeur?" she inquired, her voice a soothing whisper against the city's roar.

The young man looked up, his eyes red-rimmed. "I did something stupid," he began, a lump forming in his throat. "I YOLO'd."

Seraphel, unfamiliar with the term, tilted her head. "YOLO'd?"

Wiping away a tear, the young man elaborated, "It means 'You Only Live Once.' I took all my savings and invested them in a risky options trade, hoping to make a quick fortune." He looked towards the Bull, a symbol of financial optimism and prosperity. "I lost it all."

She sat down beside him, feeling the cool bronze beneath her. "Why take such a risk?"

He sighed, "I saw everyone around making tons of money, driving nice cars. I felt left out, like I was missing the train to success. I thought if I could just get one big win, I'd be set."

Seraphel, gazing at the Bull, understood the allure of easy wealth and the mirage of prosperity it promised. "And now?"

The young man looked defeated. "I don't know. Starting from scratch, I guess. It's just so hard when you see everyone else achieving their dreams."

Seraphel placed a gentle hand on his shoulder. "Sometimes, the most significant growth comes after a fall. And remember, not everything you see around you is as it appears."

He met her eyes, finding a depth in them that transcended the city's façade. "Who are you?"

She smiled, a touch of sadness in her eyes. "Someone who's learning that even in a city of millions, one can feel profoundly alone."

They sat there, the bronze Bull standing tall and unyielding, Seraphel realized the many faces of conquest. Here, in the heart of capitalism, it wasn't just about money; it was about dreams, gambits, and sometimes, the harsh reality of failure.

As they sat in silence, the hum of the city surrounding them, a sudden realization dawned upon Seraphel. The true conquest wasn't in toppling governments or causing natural calamities. The real conquest lay in collapsing this intricate system of illusions and facades that people so dearly clung to.

She whispered, more to herself than to the young man beside her, "If this system were to collapse, the very foundation of human society, built on dreams and aspirations, would crumble."

The young man, catching onto her words, looked up with a sudden spark in his eyes. "Collapse? You mean the financial markets? If you know something's about to happen, please, tell me!" He grew oddly animated, a stark contrast to the dejection he had exhibited moments earlier.

"Why?" Seraphel inquired, puzzled by his reaction.

He swallowed hard, gathering his thoughts. "If I knew the markets were going to crash, I could buy Put contracts. It's a way to profit from declining prices. If everything's about to fall apart, I want to be prepared."

Seraphel stared at him, taken aback by the greed masked as pragmatism. Even in the face of a potential collapse, the innate human desire to capitalize and gain took precedence.

He mistook her silence for contemplation and pleaded, "Look, if you have any information, please share. I could use a win."

Frustration bubbled within Seraphel. This world, with its intricacies and layers, confounded her at every turn. People, she realized, were bound in chains of their own making, even when faced with ruin.

She rose, her ethereal presence casting a shadow over the young man. "Your world is a paradox," she said, her voice heavy with disappointment. "In the pursuit of prosperity, many lose sight of the real treasures."

Without another word, she turned and walked away, leaving behind the bronze Bull and the young man, both symbols of a world teetering on the edge of its own desires.

# CHAPTER 25

# ENLIGHTENMENT
# AMIDST THE APOCALYPSE

Larry stood atop his familiar soapbox, his voice rising above the ambient noise of the city streets. "The end is nigh! Live now, for the Four Horsemen are upon us!"

Today was different. Not just because of the gravity of his words, but because of the silent presence that stood by him. Morten, the Horseman of Death, stood nonchalantly beside Larry, his very essence emanating an otherworldly aura. While he lacked the stereotypical cloak and scythe, anyone who dared to look into his eyes would glimpse the vastness of eternity, the finality of mortality.

For the most part, the regular pedestrians dismissed Larry as they always did. Some even chuckled, thinking Morten was simply a silent partner in today's performance or perhaps a prop to add some dramatic flair. But there was a palpable tension for those who could sense the gravitas Morten brought.

As Larry continued his proclamation, Morten's attention was drawn away from the street preacher's cries. Across the street, in a small patch of green amidst the gray cityscape, sat an individual, legs crossed, eyes closed, their breathing slow and deliberate.

Morten was intrigued. He'd seen humans in many states – in joy, in sorrow, in pain, and at the moment of their demise. But this... this was different. This human radiated an inner peace, a serenity that seemed so out of place amidst the urban chaos.

Curiosity piqued, Morten made his way towards this figure, leaving Larry to his proclamation.

Sitting on the grass, eyes still closed, the meditator sensed Morten's presence and spoke without opening their eyes. "You seem troubled, traveler. Sit. Join me in stillness."

Without quite understanding why, Morten sat down opposite the individual. The person opened their eyes, revealing irises that seemed as deep as the universe itself.

"Do you know who I am?" Morten asked, intrigued by the person's calm demeanor in his presence.

The meditator smiled gently. "It doesn't matter who you are, or who I am. In this moment, we just 'are'. Embrace the now."

The meditator's gentle words resonated deeply within Morten. "Why?" he found himself asking, unable to resist the pull of this newfound curiosity.

The meditator's eyes held Morten's gaze. "Because existence isn't just a series of events, a linear progression from birth to death. It's a collection of moments, each fleeting and precious. To be present is to truly live, to experience each of these moments in all their richness."

With an inviting gesture, the meditator motioned for Morten to sit cross-legged. "Close your eyes," they murmured, their voice a soothing balm. "Feel your breath, the ebb and flow of life within you. Let your thoughts come and go, like clouds passing through the sky. Don't hold onto them, don't judge them. Just observe."

For a while, there was only the rhythmic sound of their breathing and the distant hum of the city. But as the minutes passed, Morten grew restless. The quiet only seemed to amplify the cacophony within his mind. Thoughts about his purpose, about life and death, about the other Horsemen and the impending apocalypse, all jostled for his attention.

Unable to hold his peace any longer, Morten broke the silence. "I can't. My mind... it won't stop."

The meditator opened their eyes, offering Morten a compassionate smile. "That's natural. The mind is a curious thing. It's always in motion, always thinking, always analyzing."

Drawing a deep breath, the meditator continued, "Imagine a river. The water flows, constantly moving, constantly changing shape. It twists and turns, sometimes calm, sometimes turbulent. But through it all, it remains water. Your mind is like that river. Thoughts, feelings, memories—they're the water. They shape and reshape, but underneath it all, they're still part of the same essence."

Morten absorbed the meditator's words, the essence of the lesson still seeping into his consciousness. Taking a deep breath, he opened his eyes and rose to his feet. Gratitude filled him as he nodded at the meditator, acknowledging the precious insight he had been granted.

As he made his way back towards Larry, the world around him appeared different, as if a thin veil had been lifted. He saw the city with fresh eyes, noticing the people going about their daily lives, each individual lost in a sea of thoughts, distractions, and obligations.

A couple argued heatedly at a street corner, their faces flushed with emotion. A businessman rushed by, his focus on the phone pressed to his ear, missing the beauty of the setting sun. A group of teenagers laughed loudly, their attention more on their screens than on each other. This was the everyday orchestra of life, each person playing their part, yet missing the underlying melody.

In the midst of this, a gentle contrast caught Morten's eye. A young child was crouched down on the pavement, engrossed in the detailed examination of a solitary flower that had managed to grow through a crack in the concrete. The juxtaposition of the child's curiosity and the world's indifference was striking.

Curious, Morten approached, his attention now fixated on the scene. "What do you see?" he inquired, genuinely interested.

The child looked up, their eyes wide with wonder. "So much," came the whispered reply. "First, you see a flower. But then you see the petals, the patterns, the textures. And even deeper, there are veins, little grains of pollen, droplets of dew. Everything is so much more when you truly look."

The words resonated with Morten. This child, in their innocence, had encapsulated the essence of what the meditator had conveyed to him. Life was about truly seeing, experiencing, and immersing oneself in every fleeting moment. The flower and the river – both were metaphors for life's transience and richness.

A heavy realization dawned on Morten. The people around him, so consumed with the past and the future, were missing the gift of the present. If they weren't truly living, savoring each moment, then what was the significance of his role? How could he take away something that many didn't even recognize they had?

Morten felt the weight of a newfound purpose. He had always been a silent observer of humanity's dance, appearing only to signal its inevitable end. But what if he could do more? What if, in an effort to appreciate death, he could inspire life?

He approached Larry, whose voice was now hoarse from shouting. Larry looked at him, eyes widened in surprise as Morten placed a hand on his shoulder.

"Let me help you," Morten said, his voice carrying an ethereal power.

Larry nodded, a mix of gratitude and curiosity in his gaze.

With a deep breath, Morten stepped onto the soapbox beside Larry. The energy around them shifted, the air crackling with an otherworldly intensity.

"Listen to him! The end is nigh! I am the Horseman of Death!" Morten's voice echoed, its deep timbre resonating through the streets. Every syllable carried the weight of eons, the collective memories of every soul he had witnessed in death's void.

For a moment, the city paused. People stopped in their tracks, phones forgotten in hands, conversations silenced. Eyes turned towards Morten, drawn by an undeniable force.

Larry, seizing the opportunity, cried out with renewed vigor, "Wake up! Experience life now, for it is fleeting. Embrace every moment!"

Morten continued, "Do not wait for the end to find the value in your life. Every breath, every heartbeat, every fleeting thought... these are the moments that define existence. Don't squander them."

As the duo preached, people began to gather. Some looked on in fear, others in awe. A few began to cry, the weight of missed opportunities and unappreciated moments bearing down on them.

Amidst the gathering crowd, there were also those who started to engage with the world around them differently. Couples held each other tighter, parents hugged their children, and strangers exchanged genuine smiles. A man put away his phone and looked up at the sky, taking in the brilliant hues of the sunset. An old woman bent down to smell the roses that she'd walked past every day without noticing.

Though many had initially dismissed Larry and even the imposing presence of Morten, the message was now clear. The end might be inevitable, but the journey there was filled with endless possibilities.

Larry, panting slightly from the fervor of his proclamation, turned to Morten with a gleam of recognition in his eyes. "This is what I've been trying to tell everyone the entire time. The end is coming, and we should not be squandering the now."

Morten nodded, a strange mix of emotions playing across his ethereal face. "I know, Larry. I know."

Larry took a deep breath, looking straight into Morten's eyes. "But you, Morten? You, the very embodiment of death, preach life. Why?"

Morten's gaze softened, "Because, Larry, if people don't truly live, then death is meaningless. I am the final note in a song, the last brushstroke in a painting. Without the preceding melody or the layers of color before it, that note, that brushstroke, would mean nothing."

Larry chuckled softly, a rueful smile on his lips. "And the funny part about it, Morten?"

"Yes, Larry?"

"The funny part about it, my friend, is that we're all so terrified of you. We dread the finality of death, yet so many of us glide through life without the fear of not truly living. We're afraid of the end, but we're not afraid of the empty pages we're leaving behind. It's... paradoxical, isn't it?"

Morten smirked, the irony not lost on him. "Human nature is full of contradictions. But perhaps, with voices like yours, urging them to cherish every moment, and reminders like me, they might start to see the bigger picture."

Larry sighed, looking at the gathered crowd. "It's a start. Every revolution begins with a spark, after all. And who'd have thought? The Horseman of Death and a street preacher might just be the wake-up call this world needs."

Morten inclined his head, "Life is full of surprises, Larry."

"And so is death," Larry replied with a wink, and the two unlikely comrades turned back to the crowd, united in their mission to teach the world the true meaning of life.

# CHAPTER 26

# THE QUIET ONSLAUGHT

The chaotic energy of New York City surrounded Cassian as he navigated through the streets, his mind bustling with plans. The goal was simple: create chaos. Yet, he would soon realize that the tapestry of chaos was already intricately woven.

He started his day in a cozy café near Central Park. As he sipped on his coffee, he glanced around and caught sight of a family. Their conversation should have been filled with laughter, teasing, or even small disagreements. Instead, each face was illuminated by the blue light of individual screens. The son, the mother, the daughter—all cocooned in their digital realms. "Isolation," he murmured, ticking it off his mental list.

Wandering into a bookstore, he saw a section filled with books on conspiracy theories, self-help myths, and sensational narratives. The clerk and a customer passionately argued about a news piece they had read online. Their voices rose and fell, neither willing to consider the other's viewpoint. Cassian thought about sowing misinformation, but he found it redundant. The seeds of doubt and division had already been planted.

Exiting the store, his attention shifted to the fast pace around him. Everything was urgent—people wanted their food delivered in minutes, their packages on the same day, their desires met instantly. He had planned to intensify this urgency, but it seemed society was already suffocating from its self-created haste.

Wall Street was next. The cacophony of conversations about stocks, deals, and money engulfed him. Overhearing a young executive's conversation about her third consecutive all-nighter, he realized that the machinery of ambition had left no room for peace. Humans were burning out, consumed by their ceaseless drive.

As he ambled through the commercial district, the frenzy of consumerism struck him. A massive crowd gathered outside a store, eager for a sale to begin. Their eyes were wild, their movements frantic. The very concept of need had been replaced by the insatiable hunger for more.

Finally, in the twilight hours, he ventured into the tech hubs. Digital advertisements offered solutions for love, quantifying emotions and turning intimate moments into metrics. Humanity was reduced to bytes and bits, all neatly categorized in vast databases.

Cassian retreated to the quiet comfort of a rooftop, the city's lights sprawled before him. He had come armed with strategies, but the realization dawned that his tools of chaos were already deeply entrenched in the very fabric of human society.

Leaning against the parapet, he felt an unfamiliar emotion: a deep sense of sorrow. The people he had observed were trapped, not by external adversaries, but by their choices and desires. His role as an architect of chaos seemed almost redundant.

"They've done it themselves," he mused, staring at the glittering skyline. The city continued its pulsating rhythm, unaware that the Horseman had come and found himself unnecessary in their tale of self-inflicted chaos.

# CHAPTER 27

# The Cradle of Contrasts

Elara, the Horseman of Famine, stood on a barren hill overlooking the African savannah. Her eyes, usually glowing with an otherworldly intensity, were subdued today, clouded by a swirl of conflicting emotions.

During her travels, she saw the world, taking pauses at places of excess and indulgence. From the overflowing markets of Europe to the feast-laden tables of North America, she observed subtly, ever careful not to draw attention to her true nature. Her plan was to learn, to understand, and to strategize, all with the goal of bringing about famine.

However, today was different.

As she descended the hill and walked towards the small settlement at its base, she felt the piercing gazes of the villagers. The scene was as she expected: the fragile huts were fashioned from scrap materials, the fields were unyielding, and the skeletal livestock bore the evidence of prolonged hunger.

The villagers huddled around what little shade they could find. The sun was an unforgiving blaze in the sky, and the wind carried nothing but dust and dry heat. Children sat on their haunches, sifting through the parched earth as if expecting it to suddenly yield sustenance.

Elara stopped before a makeshift well where a woman was laboring to pull up a bucket. The bucket emerged nearly empty, carrying just a few spoons of muddy water. The woman sighed, her shoulders slumping under more than just physical exhaustion.

For a moment, Elara considered turning away, leaving this place to its suffering. What could she possibly accomplish here that wasn't already the cruel reality? But something compelled her to stay.

She approached the village elder, a man with skin like weathered leather and eyes that had long ago stopped promising better days.

"What do you see here?" he asked, surprising Elara with his English. She looked at him, momentarily at a loss for words.

"I see... I see a place that is already familiar with the work I'm meant to do," she finally answered.

"Do you find it satisfying?" he asked, peering into her eyes as if searching for her very soul.

Elara looked around at the faces of the villagers: stoic, weary, but not broken. "No," she said softly. "It's not satisfying. It's horrifying."

"Why?" he probed.

Elara hesitated. How could she explain that her purpose, her very existence, was to bring famine? But in this place, that concept lost its meaning. These people were living her mission every single day, and it was a stark mirror to what she had seen in other parts of the world. She thought of the overabundance and waste she had observed, and it filled her with a strange mix of anger and sorrow.

"Because," she finally said, her voice barely above a whisper, "I've come to realize that famine isn't something that needs to be inflicted. It already exists. And perhaps the focus should be on redirecting the abundance that exists elsewhere to places that truly need it."

The elder nodded, a subtle smile crossing his weathered face. "Even a bringer of famine can learn the value of plenty," he mused.

As Elara walked away, the whirr of her flying car's engines resonated through the air. She climbed in, casting one last look at the village below. Her destination was unclear, but her purpose had shifted, complicated by the raw truths she couldn't unsee.

# CHAPTER 28

# CONQUEST IN REFLECTION

The glow of her screen illuminated Seraphel's face as she scrolled through countless social media accounts. To understand her initial strategy better, she had started to analyze popular content on the platform. But instead of focusing on content, something else caught her eye.

Profile after profile, young women posed provocatively in their undergarments or swimwear. Some were candid, while others seemed professionally staged. A few profiles even hinted that their owners might still be in their teens. Seraphel's heart ached, and a growing sense of unease took over.

She decided to reach out to one of the young women whose vulnerability seemed apparent even through the digital medium. Tapping the direct message icon, she wrote, "Hello, I hope you don't mind me reaching out. I've come across your profile and was wondering about the reason behind sharing such personal photos. I mean no judgment, just pure curiosity."

After a few agonizing moments, a notification popped up, signaling a response.

"Who's asking?"

"My name is Seraphel. I'm new to this platform and am trying to understand its dynamics."

There was a pause before the reply came. "Fair enough. To answer your question - followers. More followers mean more popularity, which brings opportunities and validation."

Seraphel continued, "But at what cost? Aren't you concerned about the perception it might create or the negative comments?"

The reply was swift, "Every day. Every single day, I question it. But have you seen the platforms lately? This is what gets attention. As for the comments, yes, they hurt. Bullying, slut-shaming, even unsolicited advances... it's a package deal. But when the likes come pouring in, for a brief moment, the world feels alright. Comparison is the real villain here. I see other girls doing it, getting thousands of followers, leading glamorous lives. Why not me?"

Seraphel sat back, processing the weight of the conversation. "Have you ever thought of the implications of such a choice? How it might shape your future?"

A sigh seemed to emanate from the message that followed. "Of course. But in a world driven by numbers and likes, it's a risk many of us are willing to take. It's not about the present, it's about the potential. If I can turn this following into something bigger, maybe all the negativity will be worth it."

Seraphel felt a knot in her stomach. The word 'conquest' echoed in her mind. Wasn't this its very essence? The pursuit of something at the cost of everything else? "Thank you for sharing," she replied. "Your strength and candor are admirable."

The girl responded, "Thanks, I guess. Just remember, everyone has a story. Before judging anyone on this platform, it's essential to understand their why."

Seraphel locked her phone, feeling defeated. The world had already mastered conquest in ways she hadn't even fathomed. The intangible had become tangible, where validation was counted in likes and comments. As she looked at her reflection in the phone's dark screen, she felt smaller than ever, unsure of her place in a world already steeped in its own form of chaos.

The question loomed: How do you introduce conquest to a world that has already surrendered to it?

# CHAPTER 29

# AN UNEXPECTED HARMONY

The chirp of Seraphel's car communicator jolted her back to reality. The glowing emblem of the Academy projected onto the dashboard, and in a familiar voice, Ezriel spoke, "Meet at the location I'm sending. It's time."

The coordinates seemed to point towards the very edges of the Earth, a desolate spot in the Northernmost part of the planet. Thoughts raced through Seraphel's mind. But one pressing concern overshadowed everything else: Morten.

Realizing she had left him behind with Larry, she activated the car's location tracker, pulling up a map of the city. A small glowing dot, representing Morten, blinked at her from a green sprawl. The city park.

In minutes, she was hovering over the park. From above, Seraphel could spot a large gathering of people spread out on mats, moving in harmony. At the center, to her astonishment, stood Morten, guiding them through yoga poses with a calm and serene demeanor.

She landed her car at a distance, not wanting to disturb the session. As she approached, she couldn't help but marvel at the sight. Morten, the embodiment of death, was teaching people the art of living, of being in the moment, of breathing.

As the session wrapped up, many participants approached Morten, thanking him and sharing their experiences. They spoke of peace, of an intimate encounter with their fears and anxieties, and how Morten's guidance had led them to a transformative experience.

One elderly woman, her face lined with years of wisdom, said, "I've never felt so close to the end, yet so full of life. Thank you."

Morten nodded, his usually cold eyes softening. "Death is a part of life. When you embrace it, you truly begin to live."

Seraphel waited for the crowd to disperse before approaching him. "Yoga? Really, Morten?"

He turned to her, a hint of a smile playing on his lips. "Why not? When you stand at the threshold of death, you understand life in its purest form. Yoga is a celebration of that life."

She hesitated for a moment, then said, "We've been summoned, Morten. Ezriel has called."

Morten nodded, "I felt it. But I needed this, a reminder of the balance we maintain."

As they walked back to the car, Seraphel felt a newfound respect for Morten. The Horsemen, despite their missions, were still discovering the intricate tapestry of humanity. And sometimes, in the most unexpected places, they found reflections of themselves.

The car ascended, heading towards the Northern coordinates. As the cityscape shrunk beneath them, Seraphel mused aloud, "You think we can incorporate yoga into our conquest?"

Morten chuckled, "One breath at a time, Seraphel. One breath at a time."

# CHAPTER 30
# MELTING REALITIES

Inside the dimly lit halls of the Academy, Ezriel sat with Liora, an air of urgency surrounding them. The swirling portal in front of them buzzed with a life of its own, casting strange dancing lights around the room.

Ezriel held his phone in hand, his fingers hovering over the touch screen. "I need to check in on Earth," he said, his voice carrying a weight of concern.

Liora nodded, her expression empathetic. "Of course. It's been a week since you sent the Horsemen down. Let's see how things are progressing."

With a determined swipe, Ezriel pulled up his contacts and selected a name. The call connected, and as he waited for the person on the other end to pick up, the opening chords of "Take on Me" played in Ezriel's ear, and without thinking, he and Liora were both suddenly captured by the infectious melody. Their heads bobbed in unison, fingers snapping, and soon enough, they were whistling and humming along in perfect harmony, caught up in the song's tune.

The world outside the Academy's dimly lit halls seemed to fade as they became lost in the music, their urgent task momentarily forgotten. In the midst of their musical trance, Ted's voice finally broke through, his tone gently amused, "Uh, hey Ezriel, you there?"

Ezriel and Liora froze, exchanging sheepish glances as they realized they had been carried away by the song. Clearing his throat, Ezriel replied, "Uh, yes, Ted. Sorry about that."

Ted's laughter echoed through the phone, "No worries, man. You guys sound like you're having a blast. Everything okay up there?"

Ezriel managed a chuckle, his cheeks slightly flushed, "Yes, everything's fine, Ted. But I wanted to ask you about something down on Earth."

Ted chuckled, "Ah, Earth, my favorite blue marble. What's on your mind?"

Ezriel's voice turned more serious. "Ted, have you noticed anything... unusual? Signs of an impending crisis or any disturbances?"

There was a brief pause on the other end, and then Ted's voice came through, relaxed and carefree, "Nah, man. Earth's all good, you know?"

"All good?" Ezriel's tone held a hint of shock, "Last time we spoke you said that Earth was 'all good'."

Ted laughed, his voice carrying a sense of laid-back amusement, "Yeah, man. It's chill, you know. It's groovy. It's all good?"

Ezriel's brows furrowed, perplexed by the response. "You mean you're not seeing any signs of the end?"

Ted's reply was casual, "Well, I mean, everyone's got their problems, but it's all gravy, baby."

Ezriel blinked, trying to make sense of Ted's words. "Gravy? What... Ted, are you being serious?"

Ted's chuckle turned into a full laugh. "Serious? Nah, man, I'm just messing with you. Earth's Earth, you know? Same old, same old."

Ezriel was taken aback, unsure whether to be relieved or concerned. "So, you're not seeing anything unusual or out of the ordinary?"

Ted's voice was breezy, "Nah, nothing I'd call 'unusual.' Life's got its ups and downs, but it's all part of the ride, right?"

Ezriel sighed, a mix of frustration and understanding settling over him. "Yeah, I suppose you're right, Teddy. Thanks for giving me the update."

"No problem, Ezriel. Anytime you need to chat about Earth stuff, you know I'm your guy."

Ezriel smiled faintly, appreciating Ted's easygoing nature. "I'll keep that in mind. Take care, Ted."

"You too, man. Stay cosmic!" Ted's cheerful voice was the last thing Ezriel heard before ending the call.

Ezriel glanced at Liora, uncertainty in his eyes. "Well, Ted says everything's 'all good' down on Earth."

Liora raised an eyebrow, "Ted has a unique way of putting things, doesn't he?"

Ezriel nodded, his expression thoughtful. "Indeed. But I think it's time for me to check on the Horsemen personally."

Liora's gaze was steady, understanding his decision. "Be cautious, Ezriel. The Horsemen's influence can be unpredictable."

Ezriel turned to Liora, his piercing eyes softening momentarily, "Keep the Academy safe in my absence, Liora."

Liora nodded, "Always. And you, make sure you return. We still have much work to do."

With a determined step, Ezriel moved forward, plunging into the portal. He expected to feel the solid crunch of a glacier beneath his boots. Instead, there was a sensation of weightlessness, and a rush of cold air as he hurtled downwards.

He tried to reorient himself, but the stark blue of the ocean was rapidly approaching. With a tremendous splash, Ezriel plunged into the freezing waters. The chill was sharp, painful, and took his breath away. He flailed, the weight of his robes dragging him deeper into the abyss.

Just when it felt like the waters would claim him, a strong arm gripped him, pulling him upwards. Gasping for breath, Ezriel found himself face to face with Cassian, who looked a mix of concerned and amused.

"What in the seven hells are you doing? Swimming?" Cassian remarked.

Coughing and sputtering, Ezriel retorted, "There was supposed to be a glacier here!"

Hovering above the ocean, the cars looked like metallic birds suspended in the air. Elara, looking incredulous, yelled out from her window, "Is this your idea of a prank, Ezriel?"

Cassian, still dangling Ezriel out of his window, shot a glare at the soaked mentor. "Because if it was, it was a poor one."

"No," Ezriel's voice was a mix of frustration and embarrassment. "The coordinates I used were ancient, and they pointed to a vast glacier. I didn't expect... this."

Morten chimed in, "Death can be unforeseen, even for glaciers it seems."

Seraphel, ever the observer, pointed towards a distant icy structure, "There! That's where we need to go."

Without another word, Cassian, with Ezriel now safely inside his vehicle, led the formation towards the glacier. It was eerily silent, save for the hum of the engines.

# CHAPTER 31

# GLACIER GATHERING

Ezriel's piercing gaze swept across the group, a deep furrow on his forehead signaling the weight of their mission. "I called you all here to understand the progress of the Apocalypse. From what I've seen so far, I must say, Earth doesn't seem any closer to the end. In fact, I hear that Earth is 'all good'."

Seraphel, ever sharp, shot back, "Ezriel, when was the last time you've actually been to Earth?"

Ezriel paused, glancing towards the vastness of the glacier around them. "It's been centuries," he finally admitted. "But the simulator at the Academy is an exact replica of Earth's reality. And I have my sources down here."

The horsemen exchanged glances, their eyes revealing a newfound understanding that they didn't share with Ezriel. The Earth they had encountered was far from the idyllic and harmonious simulation at the Academy. They also realized that this discrepancy was their key to buying time and perhaps redefining their mission.

Elara, seizing the moment, pulled out a sleek phone. "I promised someone I'd buy a phone," she stated simply, as she flicked through image search results. She presented Ezriel with pictures of massive dams dotting America's landscapes.

Ezriel's eyebrows shot up, "Woah, Elara. This is a lot of dams...
How? Why?"

Elara's eyes sparkled mischievously, "Well, it was quite easy. You
see, humans think that dams help them, and they do in certain areas.
But then, I built thousands more, and now they're fighting for control
of the water. It's only a matter of time until the people at the bottom of
the rivers start losing all their land's resources. I may have done a lot
this week, Ezriel, but this is a long game."

Ezriel's admiration was evident, "Wow, just wow. That's genius."

Elara grinned, "And that's not all. I've poisoned their water. Over
half of private well water in the U.S. is now contaminated with PFAS."

Ezriel's eyes widened, "You poisoned their water? All in one
week!?"

Elara nodded proudly, "Yes, yes. That's exactly what I did. But
that's not even the best of it, boss. Check this out." She handed Ezriel
her phone, displaying images of disastrous famine and starvation
plaguing regions of Africa and Asia.

Ezriel was silent for a moment as he scrolled through the images,
his expression growing increasingly somber. "Elara," his tone softened,
"this is too much."

Elara's enthusiasm waned as she processed his reaction, "What do
you mean? I'm supposed to bring famine, right?"

Ezriel sighed, "No, yeah, but, like, this is way too much. You are
supposed to initiate the apocalypse, but this is just way too much, way
too quick. I mean, Elara, look at these kids, this is... a lot."

Elara's face fell, "I'm sorry, boss. I'll slow down a bit."

Cassian, sensing the opportunity, seized the phone and swiftly displayed headlines highlighting ongoing conflicts, escalating tensions between nations, and alarming statistics about the shortage of mental health professionals. "The world teeters on the edge, and the specter of war looms large."

Ezriels said, "Hold on, Cassian... is that one sovereign state encroaching upon another sovereign state?"

Cassian replied, "Well, I'm not entirely certain of the concept of a 'sovereign state,' but it appears so."

Ezriels mused, "It's as if one group of average and capable humans is invading another group of average and capable humans... quite remarkable. What's the rationale behind their conflict?"

Cassian explained, "From what I gather, one individual wants to claim ownership of the other country, while its inhabitants are steadfastly opposed, justifiably asserting, *'This is our territory. Fuck you.'* A certain bald figure, however, seems to have taken a defiant stance of *'fuck all of you,'* prompting the rest of the world to respond with a collective *'no, fuck you,'* resulting in retaliatory exchanges of *'fuck you's.'"*

Ezriel remarked, "And you facilitated all of this, Cassian?"

Cassian conceded, "Indeed, boss."

Ezriel inquired, "And what about the psychological warfare?"

Cassian replied, "Ah, yes, I've introduced mental conflict into the lives of nearly everyone. They perpetually grapple with their inner struggles. Often, they possess the knowledge to help themselves, yet they consciously opt for contrary actions... it's a peculiar kind of beauty."

Ezriel offered insight, "Impressive dedication, Cassian. Nonetheless, let's be cautious. Humans possess a formidable weapon known as 'nukes.'"

Cassian pretended ignorance, "Nukes?"

Ezriel clarified, "Yes, nuclear weapons. While your role involves bringing about the apocalypse, we'd prefer to avoid hasty annihilation. The ruination of this world should not hinge on one individual's ego or ideology."

Cassian responded, "Understood, boss. I'll bear that in mind."

Ezriel concluded, "Very well, Cassian."

Seraphel stepped forward, her gaze intense. With skillful hands, she presented infographics detailing the widening chasm of wealth, unsettling charts illustrating mounting debts, maps spotlighting borders mired in conflicts, and hidden reserves hoarded by nations. "The world remains entangled in an unending struggle for supremacy, with every nation pitted against the other."

Ezriel exclaimed, "Incredible, Seraphel. Am I interpreting this correctly? Does one percent of the U.S. population truly possess ninety percent of the country's wealth?"

Seraphel responded, "While the exact figures can vary, that's generally accurate. Approximately ninety percent of U.S. wealth is concentrated among just one percent of its population."

Ezriel mused, "It defies logic. How did you orchestrate such a scenario?"

Seraphel explained, "It was surprisingly straightforward. I simply persuaded them that wealth is the paramount pursuit in life, allowing those in power to manipulate the system in their favor."

Ezriel reflected, "A challenging endeavor, it seems."

Seraphel continued, "Indeed. And the most intriguing aspect..."

Ezriel inquired, "Yes?"

Seraphel revealed, "The most intriguing aspect is that a significant portion of the ninety percent who possess considerably less than the one-percenters actually idolize them."

Ezriel sought clarification, "What do you mean?"

Seraphel elaborated, "It's akin to those at the pinnacle claiming most of the spoils, and yet those at the base admire and aspire to emulate them. This dynamic, undoubtedly, will lead to the erosion of stability among those lower on the socioeconomic ladder."

Ezriel complimented, "Seraphel, your insight is remarkable... but about the conquest of social media."

Seraphel inquired, "Yes?"

Ezriel expressed his concerns, "Some young girls striving for followers are sharing pictures in revealing attire... even underwear."

Seraphel questioned, "Thongs... What's your point?"

Ezriel conveyed his discomfort, "It just feels ethically questionable. Don't these girls realize their images are visible to anyone? Their parents, friends' parents, educators, mentors, spiritual leaders – practically everyone."

Seraphel acknowledged, "True, some will go to great lengths in their pursuit of dominance."

Ezriel urged, "Understood, but let's remember, Seraphel, they're just young girls. Even in these dire times, let's maintain a modicum of respect."

Seraphel replied, "Noted, boss."

Morten, standing calmly in his new yoga attire, beads around his neck reflecting the subtle glow of the atmosphere, spoke with an eerie calmness, "Ezriel, death is all around us..."

Ezriel, overwhelmed with what he had seen, took a moment to absorb it all. "You've all exceeded my expectations. The Apocalypse seems imminent."

His gaze landed on Cassian. "By the way, did you meet Ted during your time here?"

Cassian's face twisted in mild disgust. "Ted... the janitor?"

Ezriel nodded, a faint smirk playing on his lips. "He's a man of many services. I thought you two would hit it off."

"Ugh," Cassian responded, clearly unamused by the revelation.

Ezriel stood up, the weight of the moment evident in his posture. Drawing a deep breath, he addressed them with a profound sincerity, his voice echoing across the vast icy expanse. "Each of you was chosen for a reason, for your unique skills and determination. While I had my reservations about letting you into a world unchecked for centuries, you have more than proven yourselves. I've always known you were capable, but today, seeing the extent of the 'change' you've brought, I'm truly in awe."

He paused, looking each of them in the eye, his gaze lingering a tad longer on Morten, who looked uncharacteristically peaceful in his new yoga attire. "Your commitment, your dedication, and your cunning... it is unparalleled. Earth stands at the precipice, and it's all thanks to you."

Morten nodded solemnly, "We merely did what we were trained to do, Ezriel."

Ezriel's eyes twinkled, and for a moment, the hard edges of the apocalypse mastermind seemed to soften. "That may be so, but I couldn't have asked for better enforcers of destiny."

With those words, he stepped back, summoning the portal with a swift motion. The swirling vortex of energy sprang to life, its shimmering surface beckoning him. "Remember, always stay true to your purpose," he said, casting one final, lingering glance at them.

As he stepped through, the portal closed behind him, leaving the horsemen alone amidst the cold, silent glacier.

For a long moment, they all stood in silence, the gravity of the situation weighing down on them. It was Seraphel who finally broke the silence. "So, I guess we can do whatever we want now?"

Elara smirked, twirling the phone in her hand, "Yeah, I mean, humanity seems to be doing fine without our intervention."

Cassian stretched, cracking his knuckles, "Guess it's time to explore some more earthly delights. Maybe I'll see what all the fuss is about with this 'sushi' thing."

Seraphel turned to Morten, "Ready to head back?"

With a serene smile, Morten replied, "Always."

The icy expanse felt somewhat warmer as the bond between the horsemen came to the forefront. They congregated, sharing firm embraces and quiet words, each realizing that their shared experience on Earth was something that would tie them together, forever.

Elara approached Cassian, a hint of mischief dancing in her eyes. "I saw the news... the Kremlin."

Cassian, ever the nonchalant one, brushed it off with a slight grin, "Oh, that. Yeah, I guess I got a little carried away."

Elara smirked, nudging him lightly. "No, no. I'm proud of you... I'm very proud of you, Cassian."

His brows quirked in surprise. "Proud? Because I saved the world from being nuked?"

"Well, that for sure," she replied, her tone turning playful, "but also... I didn't see any stabbed dicks in the footage. You didn't revert to your old tactics and... you know, stab them in their dicks, did you?"

Cassian threw his head back and laughed, "No! I guess I didn't!"

She beamed at him, "You've really grown, Cassian."

Elara hugged Cassian tightly, whispering a thank you for the moments he had saved, even if it was from impending doom he might have initiated. She then moved to embrace Seraphel, and finally Morten, each hug symbolizing gratitude and an unspoken promise of eternal camaraderie.

"Stay safe, and remember," Morten began, looking into the eyes of each of his companions, "we are always bound by purpose and fate. No matter where we go."

Cassian smiled, "Until next time."

And with that, they climbed into their vehicles. Seraphel and Morten shared a car, while Cassian and Elara each maneuvered their respective vehicles into the horizon. Their trails of departure painted the sky, signaling the close of one chapter and the beginning of another.

# Chapter 32

# Love, Hunger, and Irony

Ben stepped out of the jeep, his eyes squinting against the strong African sun. In one hand, he held a crumpled magazine. On its cover was a powerful image of Elara, her determined eyes focused on distributing food to a line of waiting children. The headline read, "Angel on Earth: The Unseen Heroine Fighting Famine in Africa.

A light breeze stirred the dust at his feet, and the distant sounds of children playing filled the air. As he looked around, his gaze landed on a familiar figure. There she was—Elara.

She looked different, more mature, worn but determined. The image of her on the magazine cover did not do justice to the raw energy and drive he could see in her now.

Elara looked up and their eyes met. A flash of recognition crossed her face, and then a playful smile. "Ben? What on earth are you doing here?"

He waved the magazine in front of her. "Saw your photo. Figured it was time to catch up. You know, since you never called me."

Elara chuckled, tucking a stray strand of hair behind her ear. "Ah, about that... I did get a phone eventually. But life here... it's been overwhelming."

Ben stepped closer, the playful tone in his voice gone. "I can see that. And I admire you for what you're doing."

She sighed. "Thanks, Ben. But honestly, I've been having this thought lately... I mean, remember when we first met? The whole romantic whirlwind, the promise of calling each other?"

Ben nodded. "Yeah, I remember thinking it was like... love at first sight or something."

Elara took a deep breath, allowing the dry air to fill her lungs, letting the moment's reality ground her. The hum of activity around them provided a stark backdrop to their conversation. "You know, I've seen mothers go without food so their children can eat, fathers walking miles upon miles just to fetch water, and communities coming together to support one another amidst despair."

She paused, her eyes distant, "In the midst of all this, where every day is a reminder of the fragility of life and the strength of human spirit, the notion of 'love at first sight' seems... trivial. It's almost disrespectful to the profound bonds forged here, based on mutual struggle and support."

Ben leaned against a nearby tree, taking in her words. "When we met, the world seemed so different. Simple even. You smile at someone, exchange a few words, and suddenly there's this... spark. But now, standing here, seeing the real challenges people face every day, that initial spark feels more like a firefly against a vast night sky."

Elara nodded, "Exactly. It's not that I don't believe in connection or even the idea of soulmates. But the fantasy of instantly falling head over heels, especially when contrasted with the raw reality around us, is... naive. Here, love is a conscious choice, an ongoing commitment. It's sharing the last morsel of food, holding onto each other during cold nights, or simply being there when all hope seems lost."

She smiled ruefully, "I mean, can you imagine? If every glance, every interaction were to be painted with the same gravity as 'love at first sight'? We'd be living in a world full of epic romances and heartbreaks at every turn."

Ben chuckled, "Sounds exhausting."

She laughed too, "Terribly so. And misleading. Love, real love, is built over time, through trials, understanding, and most importantly, through choice. It isn't just a fleeting feeling from a single encounter, no matter how enchanting."

Ben looked at her thoughtfully, "So, where does that leave us?"

Elara met his gaze, "Maybe, instead of chasing fairytales, we can build something real, grounded in this shared experience and understanding. No sparks, no fireworks, just... us."

Ben smiled, extending his hand, "I'm willing to give reality a shot."

Elara took it, "Good, because reality, as challenging as it is, has a depth and richness that fairytales can never capture."

Ben looked at her thoughtfully. "I get it, Elara. And you're right. But I'm here now, and I want to help. Maybe not as a romantic gesture, but just... as someone who cares."

Elara's face softened. "Thank you, Ben. I appreciate that."

They stood there for a moment, the weight of their surroundings pressing in, but also the comfort of a renewed friendship. Ben's unexpected arrival added a touch of lightness to Elara's mission, and together, they would continue to make a difference.

# CHAPTER 33

# UNCHARTED BATTLES

After the meeting with Ezriel and the parting of the horsemen, Cassian found himself navigating the bustling streets of New York. His usual bravado was replaced with a sense of purposelessness. War, as the world knew it, was subtly shifting from tangible battlefields to internal landscapes.

One evening, as Cassian sat on a park bench, observing humans, he noticed a woman nearby, tears streaming down her face, holding a phone and muttering, "I just need someone to talk to..." before she broke down. Cassian approached her cautiously, offering a handkerchief. She mentioned how she had been trying for months to find a therapist, but no one was available.

Curious, Cassian delved deeper into the issue. He read journals, articles, and listened to stories. The statistics stunned him: an alarming percentage of the U.S. population was grappling with mental health issues. Resources were stretched thin, and demand was outpacing supply.

He remembered the lesson from his time at the glacier: that humanity, on its own, was accelerating towards its downfall. And here, he witnessed a silent war, one that raged within the minds of countless individuals. The horseman of war realized that this was a battlefield unlike any he had seen before, one that required immediate attention.

In a cafe, Cassian overheard a group of college students discussing their psychology classes and the pressing need for more mental health professionals. An idea began to form. What if he, the embodiment of war, dove headfirst into this new battle, not as a catalyst, but as a healer?

Determined, he began to research. Cassian was unfamiliar with the world of academia and the lengthy journey to becoming a licensed therapist. However, he was a quick learner. He sourced the best books on psychology, attended open lectures, and even dared to approach some professors with questions.

While many were taken aback by Cassian's imposing appearance and intense demeanor, they couldn't deny his genuine passion. They recognized his deep understanding of conflict, and some saw potential in his unique perspective. Perhaps, they mused, this was precisely what the field needed.

It was a bizarre sight to see Cassian, the horseman of war, filling out college applications, drafting essays on the nature of internal conflict, and debating the merits of different schools' psychology programs.

Academia did not seem ready for someone like Cassian. His application essays, detailing wars across eons and how they paralleled internal struggles, were dismissed by some as fanciful fiction. Yet, one college, known for its progressive thinking, took a chance.

As Cassian attended classes, his classmates were both intrigued and intimidated. But as weeks turned into months, they saw past his stark demeanor, and witnessed a transformation. Cassian was no longer just the horseman of war; he was becoming a beacon of hope.

Professors admired his insightful contributions to discussions, linking large-scale wars and individual mental struggles. Cassian's belief, rooted in his vast experience, was clear: inside each human was a war, a battle between two wolves. And he often recited the old tale, "The one you feed wins."

His approach to therapy was revolutionary. He employed strategies from millennia of warfare, teaching individuals how to recognize and combat their internal adversaries. Instead of swords and shields, he offered tools of introspection, mindfulness, and resilience.

By the end of his academic journey, Cassian had not only earned a degree but the respect of the mental health community. His clinic, aptly named "Battles Within," became a beacon for those seeking guidance in their internal wars.

The horseman of war had found a new purpose, turning his vast knowledge of conflict into a tool for healing. And in doing so, he showcased that even the most ancient of entities could evolve and adapt to the needs of the times.

# CHAPTER 34

# MAKE LOVE, NOT WAR

Elara and Cassian were catching up over a casual brunch when Cassian seemed distant.

"Something on your mind?" Elara asked, noticing his dreamy look.

Cassian hesitated for a moment, then whispered, "I've got a janitor to go see."

"A janitor?" Elara raised an eyebrow.

"Yes, Ted... I think I've fallen for him."

Ben and Elara exchanged a knowing look. Almost in sync, they rolled their eyes.

Elara, with a teasing edge to her voice, remarked, "Met once, you say?"

Ben added, "Sounds... familiar?"

Cassian, looking slightly embarrassed but defensive, retorted, "Hey, it could happen!"

Elara's eyes widened, and a grin spread across her face, "wait… You're saying..."

Before she could finish, Morten, who had been sitting a little further away, shouted, "What did he say?"

Elara yelled back, "Cassian is gay!"

Morten, ever the hard of hearing, responded, "What?"

Elara, louder this time, "War is gay, and there's nothing wrong with that!"

"War is gay?" Morten looked surprised but then shrugged, "Of course, there's nothing wrong with that."

Seraphel, absorbed in a book, absentmindedly responded, "What?"

Morten raised his voice, "War is gay, and there's nothing wrong with that!"

Seraphel looked up, slightly startled, "Of course, there's nothing wrong with that."

The restaurant's kitchen staff chimed in, "What's that?"

Ben, sitting next to Elara, taking a deep breath, shouted, "War is gay, and there's nothing wrong with that!"

The restaurant's kitchen staff smiled, "Of course, there's nothing wrong with that."

A meditator in Tibet, hearing the distant echoes, nudged a fellow monk, "Did you hear that?"

The fellow monk, lost in thought, murmured, "What?"

"War is gay, and there's nothing wrong with that!" the meditator said.

The monk blinked, "Of course, there's nothing wrong with that."

Over in Sudan, an entire village erupted in chatter after the echoes of the news reached them. An elder, trying to get clarity over the uproar, asked, "What's everyone saying?"

A child, standing tall, responded, "War is gay, and there's nothing wrong with that!"

The elder leaned in, "Of course, there's nothing wrong with that."

Over on the West Coast, Max in California was caught off-guard by a fellow surfer who paddled by, screaming something. "What did you say?" Max shouted.

The surfer yelled back, "War is gay, and there's nothing wrong with that!"

Max shook his head, "Of course, there's nothing wrong with that."

In the Midwest, a farmer heard a passerby mention something. Turning around, he asked, "What did you say?"

The passerby shouted back, "War is gay, and there's nothing wrong with that!"

Hank scratched his head, "Of course, there's nothing wrong with that."

And finally, in the Northeast U.S., Frank shouted across his yard to his neighbor Ben, "Hey, what's everyone talking about?"

Ben yelled, "War is gay, and there's nothing wrong with that!"

Frank tilted his head, "Of course, there's nothing wrong with that."

Frank's wife, overhearing from the kitchen window, shouted, "What, hunny?"

Frank yelled back, "War is gay, and there's nothing wrong with that!"

Frank's wife shouted, "Of course, there's nothing wrong with that!"

Frank added with a smirk, "I know there's nothing wrong with it. Most of my best friends are gay."

Ben shouted, "What?"

Frank repeated with pride, "Most of my best friends are gay!"

Frank's wife, always quick with a retort, chimed in, "You don't have any friends."

Frank chimed back, "What?"

She continued, "You don't have any friends."

Frank retorted, "Well, if I did, you can bet most of them would be gay."

His wife leaned in, feigning confusion, "What?"

He emphasized, "I said, if I did have friends, they'd be gay!"

Frank turned back to Ben with a smirk, "Then maybe I'd get action more than once a year."

Ben looked at Frank seriously, taking in the joke Frank had made. "Frank," he began with a deep breath, "you realize that even if you did have a bunch of gay friends, it doesn't necessarily mean you'd get laid more, right? Being gay doesn't automatically make someone promiscuous. Gay people are just... people, with the same emotional complexities and relational challenges as everyone else. And besides," he added with a pointed look, "it would still be cheating on your wife."

Frank rubbed the back of his neck, looking a little abashed. "Yeah, you're right," he admitted. "I guess I got a little carried away."

Ben gave a small smile, "It's okay. Sometimes in the heat of humor, we might cross boundaries even without intending to. The key is recognizing it and learning."

Frank cleared his throat, "So, just to be clear, when we're saying 'war is gay', we're acknowledging that Cassian is a homosexual?"

"Yes," Ben nodded, "And there's absolutely nothing wrong with that."

Frank concurred, "Of course there's nothing wrong with that. But there is something very wrong with the act of war."

"Oh, absolutely," Ben took a deep breath before launching into his monologue, "War... war isn't gay, nor is it straight. War is this monkey-brained nonsense that perpetuates the stupidity of men killing other men for land, resources, and outdated ideologies. Instead of embracing differences, war seeks to eliminate them. It's the antithesis of love, understanding, and acceptance. It's not about who someone chooses to love; it's about the decision to hate and destroy. War is the culmination of humanity's worst tendencies, and if anything, it's the least 'human' act one can commit."

Everyone sat in reflective silence for a moment, taking in Ben's words.

Frank broke the silence, tapping his finger on the side of his glass. "Wait a minute... Ben, weren't you at brunch with Elara and Cassian at the beginning of this chapter?"

Ben looked around, confused. "Oh, yeah. I guess I was."

Frank raised an eyebrow, "And now you're here, offering wisdom on war and relationships?"

Ben shrugged, "I guess I am."

Frank smirked, "Well, that doesn't make much sense, does it?"

Ben chuckled, "No, it doesn't... But then again, many aspects of this story don't make sense."

Frank looked thoughtful for a moment, "And there's nothing wrong with that."

Ben smirked, "No, yeah. There's nothing wrong with that."

# CHAPTER 35

# A FLEETING MOMENT IN THE CITY

The city never sleeps. Skyscrapers reach high into the heavens, their tops often obscured by low-hanging clouds. Honking taxis, chattering crowds, and the distant hum of music from a rooftop bar make up the city's symphony.

Larry stood atop his usual soapbox in Central Square, a placard hanging from his neck with bold letters reading, "the end is nigh! Live now!" His frantic shouts did little to sway the sea of indifferent faces.

Just a few feet away, Morten set up his space — a serene oasis amid the chaos. Soft, ambient music played from a portable speaker, and an inviting array of yoga mats were spread out. A banner overhead read, "Embrace the Moment. Every Breath Counts."

As people passed by, Morten, donning his yoga attire and those ever-glistening beads, greeted them with a peaceful smile. "Join me, find peace within the storm," he'd often say.

At the heart of the plaza, he began his class. With his calm demeanor and soothing voice, Morten guided city dwellers through a series of poses, reminding them with each breath that life, with all its hustle, is fleeting.

After yoga, Morten organized community events – from group meditations to storytelling sessions, where people shared personal stories of moments they took for granted and lessons learned. These were instances where strangers became friends, sharing laughter and sometimes tears.

While Larry and Morten seemingly stood at opposite spectrums of approach, their message was intrinsically the same: cherish the present.

One afternoon, as Larry's voice grew hoarse from shouting, Morten approached him with a cup of herbal tea. "You know, Larry, we're not so different, you and I," he began, offering the warm cup.

Larry leaned in, smirking, "So, let me get this straight. The Horseman of Death, the guy who's supposed to be the harbinger of the end times, is here teaching the joys of life? Don't you have a boss to answer to?"

Morten chuckled, shifting a little on his mat, "Yeah, about that... Funny thing is, our earth simulator at the Apocalypse Academy is a bit... outdated. Our boss thinks Earth is way more harmonious than it actually is. I mean, I knew this place had its quirks, but... damn."

Larry's eyebrows shot up, his face a mixture of disbelief and amusement, "So, what you're saying is, you're off the hook because humans are pretty much bringing on their own apocalypse?"

Morten raised a hand, feigning innocence, "Your words, not mine... but, yeah. That's pretty much the case... for now."

Suddenly, the weight of their conversation seemed to hang in the air, heavy and soul piercing. The ever-present city noise faded into the background, leaving an almost eerie silence. They both slowly turned, eyes piercing, and stared directly at you, the reader. There was a deep, haunting resonance in their synchronized voices as they whispered, almost as a threat, "For now."

A moment passed, and then another. The world seemed to hold its breath.

And just as abruptly, Morten's face broke into a cheeky grin, dispersing the tension. "Life's a funny thing, isn't it, Larry? One moment you're an agent of doom and the next you're sitting cross-legged, teaching people to find inner peace."

Larry's eyes twinkled with mischief, "You know, Morten, sometimes life's biggest punchlines are the realities we live in."

Morten laughed heartily, "You have a point there."

Larry smirked, "Morten, do you want to get sushi and bubble tea?"

Morten's eyes brightened, "I thought you'd never ask."

# CHAPTER 36

# A GENTLE CONQUEROR

In times of old, conquest was understood as land grabs, invasions, and empire-building. But in this modern era, the nature of conquest had shifted, and so must Seraphel.

She pondered deeply on the meaning of her essence in today's world. Power dynamics, she noticed, were no longer just about land and territory, but ideas, information, and influence. Social media, technology, and globalized communication had changed the landscape of conquest. The battlefields were digital, and the warriors were influencers, CEOs, and thought leaders.

It was during one of her introspective journeys that Seraphel stumbled upon a struggling community center in Brooklyn. The place aimed to bridge the digital divide by providing access to computers and the internet for underprivileged kids, teaching them coding, digital skills, and entrepreneurship.

Watching these kids, she felt a stirring. Here was a place where she could make a difference. If conquest in this age was about information and influence, then Seraphel could empower the next generation to be the conquerors of their own destinies. But not in the destructive way conquest was once understood; this would be a gentler, more empowering form.

Using her vast resources, Seraphel renovated the center, bringing in state-of-the-art equipment. She established partnerships with tech giants, bringing in guest lecturers and mentors. Within a year, the community center was transformed into a hub of innovation and learning.

But Seraphel did more than just provide resources. She got involved personally. She organized workshops on leadership, ethical entrepreneurship, and digital citizenship. She shared stories from history, drawing parallels between ancient conquests and today's digital landscapes, emphasizing the importance of integrity, vision, and collaboration.

As word spread, more centers under the moniker "Conquest Hubs" sprouted across the country. Underprivileged kids were not only learning digital skills but were launching startups, creating apps, and becoming influencers in their own right.

The horsewoman of conquest had truly found her place in the modern world. She had reshaped the very idea of conquest, turning it from a notion of dominance to one of empowerment and positive change.

# THE LAST CHAPTER

Ezriel and Liora sat on a park bench amidst the bustling city life. The soft hum of conversations surrounded them, punctuated by the distant honks of cars and the rhythmic footsteps of joggers passing by.

Liora sipped her tea, her eyes scanning the park. "Look at them, Ezriel, all engrossed in their screens." She subtly motioned to a group of teenagers, their heads bowed, fingers swiping across the glow of their phones. "Do you think this is Seraphel's doing?"

Ezriel chuckled, "Ah, the modern conquest – not of lands, but of minds. It must be her, subtly weaving her influence."

Nearby, a couple was arguing heatedly, voices rising with each passing second. Liora shook her head. "Cassian's handiwork, perhaps? Seems like a mental war, if you ask me."

Ezriel nodded thoughtfully. "Yes, his specialty. I must say, he's refined his technique over the millennia."

They continued observing, with Liora pointing out a solitary figure on a bench, nibbling on a sandwich that looked more lettuce than anything else. "Elara?"

"Definitely," Ezriel affirmed. "A famine of flavor, it seems."

Suddenly, a distinct, peculiar aroma wafted through the air. Ezriel wrinkled his nose, glancing around. "Is that... skunk?"

Liora smirked, her nose in the air. "Not quite. It's been a while, but that's no skunk."

Following the scent, the two came across an unexpected sight. Bob Marley, alive and well, was jamming out, a doobie in hand, surrounded by a small crowd of adoring fans.

Ezriel's jaw dropped. "Bob Marley? Morten?!" His voice pitched higher in disbelief. "I know you're here, Morten!"

Liora, stifling a chuckle, nudged Ezriel. "Look further."

There, amidst a group of enthusiastic yogis, Morten stood, poised in a tree pose, his deep, calming voice guiding the participants. "Embrace the present moment, find peace in the impermanence of life."

Ezriel's gaze flitted between Bob and Morten, a mix of shock and confusion evident on his face. "Morten, the harbinger of death, teaching people to embrace life? And Bob Marley?!"

Morten, spotting the bewildered duo, gracefully exited his pose and approached them, a serene smile playing on his lips. "Ezriel, Liora," he greeted, motioning them to walk with him.

The park was alive with fleeting moments: children chasing bubbles, an elderly couple sharing a silent moment of love, and birds flitting from tree to tree. The whole of humanity, in its transient beauty, stretched out before them.

Morten gestured around, "Life, in all its glory, is impermanent. Every moment, every breath, every beat of the heart reminds us of the ticking clock. But isn't that what makes it beautiful?"

Ezriel looked at him, trying to reconcile this philosophical Morten with the Horseman of Death he had previously known. "You were meant to be the end of things, not their appreciation."

Morten chuckled, "Death is not the end, Ezriel. It's a transformation. An invitation to cherish the now. By understanding the ephemeral nature of life, we unlock a deeper appreciation for it."

Liora, looking contemplative, remarked, "And yet, society fears you."

"They fear the unknown," Morten replied, "But what is life without its inevitable conclusion? A song without its final note? A story without conclusion? It's the impermanence that gives meaning to our journey."

They paused by a pond, watching the golden hues of the sunset reflect on its calm surface. Morten continued, "By being the harbinger of death, I remind everyone to live. To embrace every laugh, every tear, every fleeting moment."

Ezriel took a deep breath, absorbing Morten's words. "I think I understand now. You've shown me a different side of the apocalypse, one where we appreciate the beauty in endings, and the promise they hold for new beginnings."

Liora nodded in agreement, "You've indeed mixed things up, Morten."

Morten smiled,. "The apocalypse is not just about destruction; it's about rebirth, renewal, and a deeper understanding of existence." He chuckled lightly, the twinkle in his eye ever-present. "Think of it this way, my friends. When plants wither away in the cold of winter, they return more vibrant in the spring, having nourished the soil from which they once sprung. Broken bones, once they mend, often grow back stronger at the fracture site. Even the harshest of winds, while they may seem destructive, actually strengthen the trees, forcing them to put down deeper roots."

# Last Chapter...
# For real this time.

Ezriel and Liora, back at the Academy and away from Earth, often found themselves reflecting on the unforeseen paths the Horsemen had chosen. Their primary mission had been unmistakable: oversee the apocalypse. Yet, what transpired was a stark deviation from the ordained plan. As days passed, a nagging anxiety settled in—what if their superiors ever caught wind of the Horsemen's antics?

One evening, amidst their shared apprehensions, Liora mused, "What happens if they ever find out, Ezriel?"

With a hint of mischief and a shrug, he quipped, "Eh, it won't be the end of the world, Liora."

Liora raised an eyebrow, "Umm... Well, it might."

Ezriel chuckled, a realization dawning on him, "Oh, true. Yes, it might."

"I have a tea for that." Liora proclaimed.

The two shared a hearty laugh, a camaraderie born of millennia working side by side. Their mirth rippled outward, a cosmic chuckle echoing across the stars, until it gently handed the reins to the narrator, who, with a throat-clearing, begins this note:

*Here, on our blue planet, nestled in the vast expanse of cosmos, humanity's existence is but a fleeting blink against eternity's canvas. Each of our lives shines briefly like a firefly's glow against the backdrop of boundless night.*

*Though we may seem inconsequential in the grandeur of the cosmos, every action, choice, and intent casts a long shadow. Wars, barriers, disagreements — these conflicts and divisions we've crafted are of our own design, while the universe endlessly whispers of unity. Humanity's unparalleled ability to create is equally matched by its propensity for destruction. Yet, amid this dichotomy lies our potential to rise, to evolve, to reimagine our purpose.*

*Humans, above all, have showcased resilience, innovation, and an undying spirit of rebirth.*

*In this story's closing moments, dear reader, we extend a heartfelt plea. Not for passive observance, but for active participation in shaping our collective destiny. Instead of ushering the apocalypse, help us break the shackles of our self-imposed limitations. Let us rewrite the future, free from the cycle of self-inflicted devastation.*

*Let's embrace each day as if it were our last. Take a moment to savor the scent of flowers, relish the touch of the breeze, and warmly greet our neighbors.*

*Rest assured, the Horsemen of the Apocalypse stand with us, championing our cause and aiding in the construction of a brighter world... for now.*

Dear Reader,

If you're reading this, then it's safe to say we've managed to dodge the apocalypse—for now, at least. The world may have seen its fair share of chaos and calamity, but here you are, flipping through these pages and proving that a good sense of humor can survive just about anything.

We want to express our sincere gratitude for joining us on this comedic journey. Your presence and support have meant the world to us. Your laughter has been the driving force behind our pen, and we're grateful for the chance to share a few chuckles in these uncertain times.

Thank you for reading.
*Nitka Marga*

# NITKA MARGA

Nitka Marga is a comedic wordsmith with a twist. While he delves into the darker realms of comedy, his works are imbued with hope, positivity, and spiritual insights. Nitka writes to unravel the mysteries of the human condition and inspire readers to uplift their spirits.

**Writing Style:** Nitka's signature style combines humor with spiritual wisdom, offering readers a one-of-a-kind perspective that both entertains and enlightens. His narratives empower readers to find humor in life's chaos while discovering deeper truths about themselves.

**Exploring the Human Condition:** Nitka's writing mission is to entertain and provide fresh perspectives that empower his readers. His works serve as windows into the human experience, helping individuals navigate the complexities of existence with laughter and introspection.

**Diverse Literary Terrain:** In addition to his contributions to the realm of comedy, Nitka extends his literary craft to spiritual fiction, weaving narratives infused with profound insights derived from yoga and ancient philosophies. His repertoire also includes publications in self-help and empowerment, providing readers with tools and perspectives to navigate life's challenges and embrace their own journey with wisdom and resilience.

# Happily Never After

a journey through
## FAIRYTALE REHAB

NITKA MARGA

Release Date: October 30th, 2023

In a world where fairy tales don't always end in "happily ever after," the characters we've loved from our childhoods find themselves grappling with the complexities of reality. Dive into an enchanting tale where iconic figures embark on a transformative journey inside the Ever After Sanctuary. Under the watchful eyes of Dr. Chronos, the White Rabbit, and with the magic of the sanctuary, they confront their past traumas, rediscover their authentic selves, and strive for redemption and self-awareness. From the misunderstood Big Bad Wolf to the enigmatic Frog Prince and Princess, Nitka Marga crafts a poignant narrative of resilience, compassion, and the quest for a different kind of happy ending.

Join these characters as they unravel their stories, face their fears, and seek the healing they deserve. "Happily Never After" is a testament to the power of understanding and the boundless nature of the human (and fairy tale) spirit. Don't miss this fresh twist on timeless tales.

**Warning:** This isn't your standard fairy tale book. Packed with edgy humor and sharp wit, "Happily Never After" is not for the faint of heart. Expect audacious jokes, vulgar humor, and a sprinkling of coarse language. This compelling adventure beckons you to look beyond the sanitized sweetness of modern storybook versions, inviting you to explore the gritty and raw aspects of characters you thought you knew.

NITKA MARGA

www.ingramcontent.com/pod-product-compliance
Lightning Source LLC
Chambersburg PA
CBHW020246130626
46549CB00005B/2094